KC's han _____ ge.

"It's from the housing office," she told Winnie through gritted teeth. "It has, quote, come to their attention that I have an illegal roommate. I have one week to *rectify the situation* before they *take action.*" She thrust one of the pieces of paper under Winnie's nose. "Here's the copy of the letter that informed on us. Look at the signature."

Winnie's worried eyes focused on the letter. Then she gasped. "I don't believe it. *Brooks Baldwin?*"

"Why is he doing this?" KC shouted. She was so angry that she kicked the metal garbage can, sending it skidding across the floor. "He's ruining my life. He broke up my relationship with Cody. He tried to get me fired. Now he's trying to get me thrown off campus."

"What are you going to do?" Winnie asked.

KC took a deep breath and struggled to get her temper back under control. "I don't know," she said in a shaking voice. "But it's time to start fighting back. Time to let the world know what kind of sick, evil person Brooks really is."

Don't miss these books
in the exciting FRESHMAN DORM series

FRESHMAN FURY

LINDA A. COONEY

HarperPaperbacks
A Division of HarperCollins*Publishers*

This is a work of fiction. The characters, incidents, and
dialogues are products of the author's imagination and are not
to be construed as real. Any resemblance to actual events or
persons, living or dead, is entirely coincidental.

HarperPaperbacks *A Division of* HarperCollins*Publishers*
10 East 53rd Street, New York, N.Y. 10022

Copyright © 1993 by Linda Alper and Kevin Cooney
Cover art copyright © 1993 Daniel Weiss Associates, Inc.

All rights reserved. No part of this book may be used or
reproduced in any manner whatsoever without written
permission of the publisher, except in the case of brief
quotations embodied in critical articles and reviews. For
information address HarperCollins*Publishers*,
10 East 53rd Street, New York, New York 10011.

Cover illustration by Tony Greco

First printing: November, 1993

Printed in the United States of America

HarperPaperbacks and colophon are trademarks of
HarperCollins*Publishers*

❖ 10 9 8 7 6 5 4 3 2 1

One

Click.

". . . lots of rain this morning. If you gotta be out there, wear a smile. But take an umbrella, too. Now let's have a little music . . . Here's 'Cloudy Over You,' a new release from the same folks who recorded 'Heartbeat' last summer . . ."

KC Angeletti's eyes flew open and she jerked awake as her subconscious identified the familiar voice on the clock radio. It was early Saturday morning and the room was still dark. And chilly. And damp.

KC shivered and wrapped her quilt around her as she reluctantly rolled out of bed and put her bare feet on the cold floor.

Slowly and carefully she began picking her way across the room to the clock radio that sat on the edge of the built-in white Formica desk on the other side of the room. Its green face glowed in the dark.

KC's single study dorm room in Langston Hall was small to begin with. And since her old friend, Winnie Gottlieb, had moved in with piles of her own possessions, it had become unbearably crowded. Crossing the room was like trying to get across an obstacle course.

Winnie had recently split up with her husband, Josh Gaffey, after a short but emotionally turbulent marriage. During that time, Winnie had gotten pregnant, had a miscarriage, and seen Josh transfer his affection to another girl named Fredi Barstow. Her stay with KC was supposed to be temporary—just until she could get her act together and find another place to live. But so far, Winnie hadn't been very aggressive about looking.

Winnie had started out staying with Faith Crowley. Faith, Winnie, and KC had been best friends since the ninth grade. Faith was the motherly one of the three, KC reflected as she stepped carefully. The nurturing one. The understanding one. She had always been better at coping with Winnie than KC had, and KC briefly fantasized about sending Winnie back to Faith's room.

All three girls had come to the University of

Springfield together, but they had made a point of trying to live in different dorms. KC had chosen a single study room in Langston Hall because it promised its residents few distractions, long quiet hours, and an atmosphere in which to pursue a serious course of study.

Now here she was with a huge distraction called Winnie Gottlieb—right in the middle of her austere, purposely unadorned sanctuary.

"Ouch!" KC winced as her foot came down on something sharp. Then she let out a little yip of alarm when her other foot tripped over Winnie's sleeping body. She took a few quick steps to regain her balance and in the process stepped on a lipstick, a hairbrush, and felt the soft squish of a sandwich under her heel.

Ugh! Why did Winnie have to be such a slob? The room was a mess. KC's eyes were adjusting to the dark now and she glared down at Winnie's inert body. Winnie hadn't even stirred. But her sleeping face looked so sweet and childlike, KC felt some of her annoyance slipping away. Winnie was trying to be a good houseguest. She really was. But there was just something in her DNA that completely resisted KC's everything-in-its-place philosophy.

The voice of the announcer came back on the radio, rekindling some of her irritation. Winnie had set the alarm last night. How could she have left it tuned to KRUS, the campus station? She knew that KC's former boyfriend, Cody Wainwright, did the wake-up show. Winnie had just been through a breakup herself. How could she be so thoughtless? Would Winnie want to wake up to Josh's voice?

KC quickly reached out toward the radio to change the channel. But the soft Tennessee accent and mellow timbre of Cody's voice sounded so comforting and familiar, she couldn't bring herself to turn him off. Instead, she lowered the volume, sank down into her desk chair, and listened.

There was an easy, relaxed charm about Cody's personality that perfectly suited him for his job as a campus radio DJ.

She couldn't believe how much she missed him. Hearing his voice brought everything back—his smile, his hugs, his good-humored teasing. How could she ever have thought he would betray her? She must have been crazy to accuse him of turning her in to the Secet Service investigator.

Not long ago, KC had stupidly let herself get involved in a long-distance phone-calling scam. She had made dozens of long-distance calls and used a phony credit-card number to avoid having to pay for them.

She wasn't proud of herself for what she had done. But when Cody found out about it, he had made her feel even worse by insisting that she confess her role to the phone company's investigator and make some effort to repay them.

Cody was into honesty in a big way. But instead of listening to Cody and approaching the phone company about making restitution, she had waited for them to track her down. And they had. *With the help of an informer,* they had told her.

For some insane reason, KC had decided that the informer had to be Cody. She had slapped his face in public and said every scathing thing she could think of.

Later, when she had come to her senses and realized that Cody would never betray her that way, it was too late. Cody was angry, disappointed, and pretty clear about not wanting to see her again.

". . . don't get mad at the rain . . ." he was saying. ". . . if we didn't have a monsoon season here in Springfield, we wouldn't have Bumbershoot. That's right. 'Bumbershoot' means umbrella, but it's also what we call our annual two-week festival held in honor of the rain. Pick up a list of events at the Student Union today. There are two big dances, exotic foods, a visit from a famous humorist, and a grand finale Rain or Shine picnic at Mount Crinsley. Rain or shine, we'll be having a picnic and bluegrass concert. Sound nuts? Well, sure. But that's what Bumbershoot is all about."

KC listened to the enthusiastic announcement with a mixture of longing and regret. All those events would be fun to attend with Cody. KC wondered if he was thinking of her as he read off the list of entertainments. Wondered if he was missing her as much as she was missing him.

The light rain outside made a steady drumming sound against the window. As the dawn broke, KC saw the white tips of the mountain peaks that lay in the distance. The tallest of them was Talisman Rock. It was a tough peak for climbers, but the lower mountains, like Mount Crinsley, were full of picnic areas and romantic walking paths for lovers.

KC turned and studied her reflection in the mirror. Cody had always admired her dark, classic beauty, her tall, model-thin figure, her cool and elegant walk. She pushed the long thick hair back from her forehead and held it high. He'd seen her with her hair up once and complimented her. He'd complimented her on so many things during their relationship—her initiative, her business smarts, her drive—it was hard to believe he was really prepared to walk away for good.

"What are you doing up so early?" asked a sleepy voice from the floor.

"I have a job interview this morning, remember?"

"Oh yeah," Winnie said with a yawn. She sat up and stretched her arms high over her head. "Yuck!" She grimaced, looking out the window. "If I were you I'd blow it off and go back to bed. Looks pretty dreary out there."

"I wish I could," KC said, snapping off the radio and picking up her hairbrush. "But I owe

the phone company three hundred and seven dollars for those long-distance calls I made. If I don't pay it, they'll press criminal charges."

Winnie smacked her lips sleepily. "I wish I were really rich. Then I'd give you three hundred and seven dollars so you could go back to bed."

KC laughed and felt all of her annoyance go away. If Winnie were rich, she would indeed give KC three hundred and seven dollars. She would give KC anything she asked for. Winnie had always been generous with what she had. "I wish you were really rich too," KC said. "I wish *I* were really rich."

Unfortunately, KC was far from wealthy. In fact, unlike Winnie and Faith, KC was poor. Her parents were former hippies who had run a health-food restaurant when her dad had been alive. He had passed away several months ago and now her mother was living in Montana, trying to make a go of an old dude ranch.

There had never been any extra money around the Angeletti household. Being constantly broke had never seemed to bother her parents. But it had bothered KC a lot. And it had inspired her with a real determination to get ahead in the world.

"You'll be rich someday," Winnie assured her with a sleepy smile. "So where is your interview? Get Rich Quick, Inc.?"

KC laughed. "No such luck. I'm going to see

Eric Hindemann at Mountain Supply."

"The sporting-goods store? You're kidding," Winnie exclaimed. "That Eric Hindemann has a terrible reputation. He's supposed to be a real tyrant."

KC nodded. "I know. But that's good, because it means there's a lot of turnover. People are always getting mad and quitting. That's why there's almost always a job opening there."

"I thought you applied for a job there once before," Winnie said. "At the beginning of the year."

KC went over to the dresser and opened one of the drawers. Her wardrobe wasn't extensive, but the few things she had were classic and well-made. Since it was rainy and unseasonably cool today, she chose a dark-green cable-knit sweater to wear over pressed khakis. It looked outdoorsy and casual, which was not the way she would usually dress for a job interview. But today it was right on target. "I did," she said to Winnie as she took off her nightgown. "But he wanted somebody with a lot of outdoors experience, not a business major."

Winnie laughed. "Have you recently acquired some outdoors experience that I don't know about?"

"Well, I have been outdoors a lot," KC responded with a smile.

"Yeah. Sunbathing." Winnie giggled.

"Well, maybe I haven't had any outdoors experience," KC said seriously. "But I'm hoping I can persuade him to give me a chance. I don't have to last long in the job—just long enough to make three hundred and seven dollars."

Winnie sat up and ran her fingers through her spiky hair. It looked to KC as though she had slept in her eye makeup again. Dark streaks of mascara ran from her eyelids to her chin. There also appeared to be some food stuck to her cheek.

KC sighed. Sometimes having Winnie for a best friend was like having a child. A manic, kooky, self-destructive, running-off-in-six-directions-at-once child. There was no sense in getting mad, she reminded herself sternly. That was just Winnie. "Winnie," KC said in a patient voice, "what's with the food all over the place?"

"I lost my nonresident Dining Commons pass," Winnie admitted. "So I'm sort of living on junk food and vending-machine sandwiches until my mom sends my allowance and I can get a new pass."

KC rolled her eyes and reached for her purse. "Here," she said, whipping her own card out. "Use mine and get yourself a decent breakfast."

"What about you?"

KC looked at the clock. "I don't have time. I want to be at Mountain Supply when it opens."

Winnie gave KC a crooked smile. "Thanks, KC," she said in a small voice. "And good luck."

KC shrugged herself into a rain slicker, grabbed the umbrella that leaned in the corner, and hurried out into the hall. A thin layer of dried mud and leaves covered the carpeted floor—evidence of the heavy rains that had turned large sections of the campus into a boggy quagmire.

Fortunately the rain had slacked off to a drizzly mist by the time KC stepped outside. She inhaled deeply. The mountain air had that weird, could-be-fall, could-be-spring feeling. Chilly, but without the sharp edge. Lots of students seemed to be dressed for both seasons at once—wearing shorts with their sweaters and heavy boots as they hurried along the puddle-covered sidewalks that connected the campus buildings.

KC cut diagonally across the dorm green and hurried down the sloping lawn that led to the wide boulevard bordering the campus. There was very little traffic at this hour and a bus was waiting there already. KC hopped on and paid her fare. Within minutes, it seemed, the bus was pulling up to the downtown shopping district. KC stepped off in front of the huge sports boutique that was known as Mountain Supply. The front of the building had been faced with split logs so that it had a rustic look. In the display window, a tent and various types of outdoor equipment had been set up to resemble a campsite. In the corner, a large stuffed bear stood up on its hind legs and looked out on the sidewalk.

Hurrying inside, KC immediately recognized the tall, redheaded man with a beard who was unlocking the cash register. It was Eric Hindemann. His face wore its customary sour expression.

KC squared her shoulders and cleared her throat as she approached him. "Excuse me . . ." she began.

"Yes," he said curtly. Obviously he didn't remember her. He looked so unfriendly and uninterested that it momentarily shook KC's confidence. She looked around the store at the piles of equipment. What was all this stuff, anyway? What was it for? What did it do? Even the clothes looked strange and unfamiliar. Was she crazy? How could she sell merchandise if she didn't even know what it was?

"Young lady," Mr. Hindemann barked, "I have a lot to do. Did you want something?"

KC's jaw dropped. Boy! He was even ruder than she remembered. What kind of businessman was he? Didn't he know better than to treat potential customers this way? His arrogant disregard for the principles of sound business practice offended her to the very core of her bones. Job or no job, Eric Hindemann needed a lesson in retailing.

Her brows lifted coolly. "Yes. I would like to buy three thousand dollars' worth of sporting goods."

Mr. Hindemann's eyes brightened and his

mouth fell open. "Are you serious?" he breathed.

KC's brows snapped together over the bridge of her nose. "No," she barked. "But what if I were? Do you really think I'd still be standing here ready to spend my money after the way you spoke to me? Heck, no. I'd be out looking for another sporting-goods store. And when I found one, I'd spend *four* thousand dollars, just to spite you."

Mr. Hindemann's face turned an angry purple. "Who are you?" he demanded.

"I'm KC Angeletti. I'm a freshman business major at the University of Springfield. I've spent my whole life in retail business—food, clothing, calendars—and I think you need somebody like me."

"I do not need somebody like you," Mr. Hindemann argued.

"Anybody that just lost a three-thousand-dollar sale needs all the help he can get," KC shot back.

Mr. Hindemann's mouth opened and closed several times as he struggled to express the depths of his outrage.

KC stared blandly at him with one eyebrow slightly cocked.

Mr. Hindemann sputtered for a moment, then suddenly he began to laugh. "All right. All right. You made your point. But I'm still not in the market for any business majors—unless they know sports equipment. I need somebody who knows rafting, skiing, climbing. You know anything about those sports?"

"Selling is selling," KC insisted. "And I can learn. Besides, I spoke to one of your ex-employees at the Student Union a couple of days ago. He said that the rainy season is always slow for this store. That means I'll have some down time to familiarize myself with the merchandise. It also means I would have a little time to think up a promotion—something to do with the rain. Maybe some rain product that everybody will want."

Mr. Hindemann nodded. "You're persistent, and I like that. But I don't just need salesmanship and fancy business-school promotional ideas. I need good, old-fashioned trustworthiness, too." He darted his eyes around the store as if looking for shoplifters. "I get a lot of shrinkage in here when I hire students."

KC drew herself up. "I assure you, Mr. Hindemann, no one has ever been given any reason to doubt the trustworthiness of KC Angeletti." Behind her back, her second and third fingers were tightly crossed. She was taking a big chance. If Hindemann found out why she was so eager for this job, he would boot her out on her ear.

Hindemann sighed. "Stick around for an hour or so and I'll give you a trial run." He gestured toward the door with his head. "Here comes somebody now. Why don't you see if you can move some of the rock-climbing equipment?"

With that, he turned on his heel and disappeared down an aisle stocked with weights.

Rock-climbing equipment? What did that mean? KC's eyes flew around the store looking for clues, then rested on a huge poster depicting a well-built young man making his way up the face of a sheer cliff. KC recognized that cliff. It appeared on several of the University of Springfield postcards, recruiting materials, and calendars. It was Talisman Rock.

IF YOU'RE GOING TO THE TOP, read the bold-faced type below the climber, GO WITH CRAMPONS.

KC turned back toward the door and some of her nervousness began to subside. The customer was Brooks Baldwin. She and Brooks had known each other for years. They had gone to high school together.

"Hi, Brooks," she said enthusiastically. "What are you doing in here?"

It was a silly conversational gambit. Brooks lived in Rapids Hall, the outdoor-pursuits dorm. He was always rafting or climbing or playing rugby. Mountain Supply was probably one of his regular hangouts.

As usual, he was dressed in hiking boots and jeans. The white collar of his rugby shirt was tucked into the neck of his brown crewneck sweater. His curly blond hair was curlier than usual from all the humidity. And his ruggedly handsome face wore a distracted frown. When he looked at KC, it seemed to take him a moment or two to focus and realize who she was. His tanned face broke into a tentative smile. "Hi, KC."

It seemed to KC that she was seeing that expression on Brooks's face a lot these days—ever since he had started dating Angela Beth Whitman. If anyone could make a man look melancholy, confused, puzzled, and distracted, it was definitely Angela Beth. She was a shapely brunette with a dazzling smile and an abrasive personality. Any man who loved Angela Beth, KC reflected, was in for a bumpy ride. Beautiful and sexy, but petulant and demanding. KC had seen Angela Beth in action a couple of times. Angela Beth was a member of the Gammas and KC was a member of the Tri Betas. The two sororities were fiercely competitive, and KC knew from experience that Angela Beth could be ruthless when it came to getting what she wanted.

KC almost felt a little sorry for Brooks. Especially when she noticed that his broad shoulders were looking a little slumped. Dating Angela Beth was probably pretty exhausting.

"I just thought I'd come in and take a look around," Brooks said flatly.

KC threw another look at the poster on the wall. "Been to the top of Talisman Rock yet?" she asked.

That drew a smile. "Can't say that I have. That's a pretty tough climb."

"Not for somebody like you," KC protested. "Not if you had the right equipment."

Brooks reached around and rubbed the back of his neck. "I guess." His attention was wandering and his voice was weary and uninterested.

"I heard Angela Beth climbs too. Maybe you could climb it together. The Bumbershoot picnic is coming up. That would be a great time to scale to higher ground."

Brooks smiled. "I probably could, but I don't think Angela Beth's equipment is up to a climb like that."

"Then why don't you treat her to some crampons?" KC suggested.

Brooks frowned. "Get her crampons for a present? I don't know. It doesn't seem like a very romantic present to give a girl."

"Are you kidding? Two people making their way together up an icy cliff, hearts pumping, muscles straining, one hand reaching out to clasp another . . ."

Brooks looked startled, and KC wondered if she was overdoing it. Then his eyes sort of clouded over as if he were picturing it. "Yeah," Brooks breathed. "Yeah. You're right, KC. I should get Angela Beth some crampons."

A little smile played around the corner of KC's lips. Brooks was a straight-A student, but he was amazingly easy to manipulate.

"You'd need a pick, too," she said, glancing

again at the poster.

"I think you mean an ice ax."

"An ice ax," KC corrected.

"And gloves," he mused.

"And gloves," KC agreed eagerly.

Brooks pulled his wallet from his back pocket and opened it. "I may not have enough cash on me," he murmured as he thumbed through the folds of the wallet.

"We'll be happy to take a check if you have a validated student ID," said a deep voice behind KC.

She and Brooks looked up and saw Mr. Hindemann smiling benignly. "I did hear you say you wanted some crampons, an ice ax, and some gloves, correct?"

Brooks blinked. "Yeah. That's right."

"If you'll follow me, I'll ring you up over at this counter." Mr. Hindemann gave KC an almost imperceptible wink and led Brooks down aisle five. KC scurried behind and watched with interest as Mr. Hindemann packed up the merchandise she had sold. *So those are crampons,* she thought as he placed some metal cleats in the box.

Brooks handed Mr. Hindemann a check for the total and lifted the large box off the counter.

"Let me help you carry that to your car," KC offered quickly.

Together she and Brooks carried the things to the parking lot. The rain was still holding off and the sun was shining down on the pavement, drying the puddles in the black asphalt parking lot. Brooks opened the trunk of his car and placed the box in the back. "Thanks for the gift ideas," he said, smiling.

His face was so open and trusting, it made KC feel a little guilty. "Ah, listen, Brooks. I think I should tell you—I was auditioning for a job in there. Trying to show Mr. Hindemann that I could sell sports equipment even though I'm not athletic."

Brooks looked confused for a moment, then he threw back his head and began to laugh. "You are too much, KC! Boy, you really got me. Two months' allowance gone like . . ." Brooks snapped his fingers.

KC laughed too. One thing about Brooks, he was always a good sport. A lot of people would have been angry with her. "Audition or not," she choked. "I stand by my suggestions. That's a great gift for a girl like Angela Beth. She'll love it."

Brooks put his hand on KC's shoulder. "You're right. And even if she doesn't, I promise not to bring all the equipment back. I'm glad I had a chance to help you." He opened the door and sat down in the driver's seat. "As I'm sure you've probably figured out, I was the one who turned you in to the phone company."

A shrieking alarm bell went off in KC's brain.

What did he say?

His face clouded over. "I can't really explain why I did it, but I've felt really bad about it. I'm glad it didn't cause any big trouble for you." He jerked his back toward the trunk and grinned. "We'll call ourselves even from now on."

KC's mouth was hanging open. There were so many things she wanted to scream at him, she didn't know where to start. How could he stand there smiling at her as if everything was fine between them? Didn't he have any idea how much damage he had done?

Brooks shut the door and started the engine. "Thanks again, KC."

The engine roared and the car pulled out from the between the parallel parking lines just as KC was finding her tongue. *"You . . ."* she began.

"KC," she heard Mr. Hindemann call.

She looked up and saw him smiling at her from the end of the parking lot. "Are you going to stand there all day or are you going to get back to work?"

KC stared dumbly at him.

"You're hired," Mr. Hindemann said. "But on a two-week trial basis. You did a good job with that sale. But you mess up and you're fired."

Mr. Hindemann disappeared around the corner of the building and KC hurried to follow. Her mind wasn't on sporting goods, though. It was on Brooks Baldwin and his cruel betrayal.

Two

"**M**an! It's coming down like cats and dogs out there." Ted Markham made a big show of shivering and hugging Faith tightly against his chest.

They were sitting on his brother, Danny's, bed, and leaning against the wall next to the window with textbooks in their laps. Faith pressed her face into the shoulder of Ted's bulky blue sweater and returned the hug. Her own sweater was an open-work crochet, cinched at the waist with a silver concho belt, and not quite warm enough with the faded denim cutoffs she wore with it. She smiled. It didn't matter, with Ted sitting next to her. Ted was tall and athletic and radiated warmth—

physical and emotional. In spite of his extensive character flaws, he made her happier than any guy she had dated since the beginning of her freshman year.

Ted was blond and blue-eyed. Faith's hair was a darker, honey-colored blond, and she wore it in a long, loose braid. Like Ted, her eyes were blue. But they were a sincere, cornflower blue. The kind of blue that inspired trust and made people feel at ease. Ted's eyes were a crackling periwinkle that teased and challenged.

He hugged her again and Faith giggled. "Does this look like studying to you guys?" she said.

Dash Ramirez and Lauren Turnbell-Smythe sat on the floor of Danny's single dorm room, poring over Lauren's notes for their next newspaper column. "No, it doesn't," Lauren said sternly. "It looks like snuggling."

"I thought the rules were clear to everyone," Danny said from his wheelchair. He lifted his eyes from his art-survey textbook and stared disapprovingly at his brother. "No snuggling until the bell."

Danny's girlfriend, Melissa McDormand, looked up from her own seat at Danny's desk. "Snugglers will be prosecuted," she said in a prissy voice.

Like Ted, Danny was blond and blue-eyed, but his hair was on the shorter side. He was muscular and athletic, and the well-developed muscles of his broad chest and shoulders stretched against the fabric of his navy and red striped long-sleeved polo shirt. His lower half, paralyzed from a car accident, was clothed in bulky gray sweatpants.

Faith chuckled and Ted released his grasp. "Okay, okay," he said, pretending to pout. "I'm studying. I'm studying." He darted a look at Lauren and Dash. "Boy! This is the biggest bunch of study grinds I've ever met. Am I the only one who realizes that it's Saturday night?"

Danny shook his head. "Now, Ted," he said in the deep voice of a TV-sitcom dad, "an education is not to be wasted. You can't spend all your time chasing girls and playing Frisbee. That's why your mother and I have decided to send you to military school."

The group burst into laughter.

"You're a great mimic, Danny," Lauren said. "And the things you say are always funny. You should be on stage."

Before Danny could respond, the alarm clock went off, signaling that the study portion of the evening was over.

"Party!" everyone shouted, tossing papers, pens, and notebooks into the air.

"Snuggle time!" Ted said, pulling Faith's head down on his shoulder.

"Snack time!" Dash announced, producing a box of doughnuts.

"News flash!" Lauren announced. "And boy, have I got a story."

There was a flurry of activity as everybody tucked their study materials into backpacks and settled themselves comfortably around the room.

"Okay, shoot," Dash said, reaching for a doughnut. He stuck the doughnut in his mouth and wiped his fingers on the tail of his ink-stained T-shirt. Dash was a sophomore journalism major, and a reporter and columnist for the University of Springfield newspaper. His hair was dark and shaggy and held in place with a blue bandanna tied in street-gang fashion.

His girlfriend, Lauren, a freshman and fellow newspaper writer, crossed her jean-clad legs. The damp weather caused her fine blond hair to appear even finer than usual, but it made her pale, porcelain complexion look dewy and flawless. "I saw KC this afternoon, and she's gotten a job at Mountain Supply. Her first customer was Brooks. Turns out it was Brooks who informed on KC to the phone company."

Melissa and Faith exchanged glances.

"You're kidding," Faith said. "I mean, that's not the kind of thing Brooks would do."

Brooks had been Faith's friend since grammar school, and her boyfriend all during high school. She had broken up with him soon after arriving at the U of S. Brooks was solid and dependable and responsible and everything a girl was supposed to want, but there had been something missing in their relationship. Whatever that something was, Faith thought she had found it with Ted—which was pretty unbelievable, since Ted was notorious all over campus as a chaser, cheater, and charmer.

Very quickly Lauren filled the group in on what Brooks had said to KC.

Dash reached behind his head and tucked the ends of his bandanna up. "So she never got a chance to tell him off?"

"No," Lauren said. "But she told me she's going to let him have it when she gets hold of him." She took off her wire-rim glasses and rubbed her fatigued violet eyes. "She looked pretty frazzled when I talked to her," Lauren went on. "Like if Brooks came along she might go berserk. I think the pressure of trying to come up with that three hundred and seven dollars has really gotten to her. And finding out that Brooks ratted on her was a real blow."

Faith fiddled with the silver conchos on her belt. "She's been through a lot over the last couple of months."

"Let's face it," Dash said. "We're all closer to the edge than we like to think. The pressures of college life can be overwhelming." He groaned and fell back on the floor so that his head landed in Lauren's lap. "Take me and Lauren. We live with constant deadline pressure." He gazed up at

Lauren. "Let's not be newspaper writers anymore. Let's be park rangers."

There were shouts and hoots of laughter. Lauren and Dash's last column had been a hilarious account of their ill-fated camping trip. "Ha, ha," Lauren replied dryly. "You, me, and nature are not a good combination. And speaking of nature," she said to the rest of the group, "Cody Wainwright wants me and Dash to work up some kind of comedy routine for his Bumbershoot broadcast from Mount Crinsley. The Rain or Shine picnic. We're supposed to be Gustav and Alice Mulch."

"The Nature Twins." Dash grinned, sitting up. "He got the idea from our camping column."

"That column was a scream," Melissa hooted. "When are we going to see another one?"

"Arrgghh!" Dash and Lauren both wailed together.

"According to our editor, Greg Sukamaki, in two weeks," Lauren moaned.

"But don't hold your breath," Dash said. "Because so far neither one of us has had a good idea for another humor piece."

Melissa whistled. "I don't think I could live with that kind of pressure."

"We're *all* under pressure," Dash repeated, sitting up and warming to his subject. "Look at you. Track scholarship. How many of us could live with that kind of pressure? *Win that race or leave school*. And Ted—he's got an important assign-ment for his media class, and not a clue about what he's going to do."

"Don't remind me," Ted groaned.

"Faith, you're a theater major and you're studying to be a director. But you know directors are only as good as their last show. The pressure is always on to do it again—and do it better than the last time. And Danny . . ."

"Stop! Stop!" Danny screamed, holding his head in mock despair.

"Group groan!" Ted announced.

"Arrggghhhh!" they all wailed at once.

Faith stared at the circle of friends with real ap-preciation. Every face was twisted into a parody of horror and fear.

Dash stood and pulled Lauren to her feet. "Come on, Alice Mulch. Study time is over and it's time to blow off a little steam to relieve the pressure."

He snapped his fingers at Ted and Faith, and then at Melissa and Danny. "You guys, too. Come on. Everybody up and at 'em."

"Where are we going?" Faith asked as Ted helped her to her feet.

"Yeah, Dash. Where are we going?" Ted asked.

"Tonight's the first Bumbershoot Dance at the gym. And it should be starting right about now."

"All right," Ted said, signaling his approval by twirling Faith around behind him. Faith smiled, laughing until she caught sight of Danny and Melissa. *A dance!* Suddenly she felt ashamed. It was such a simple thing, going to a dance. Simple for her. Not simple for Danny.

Without thinking, she flexed the muscles in her legs, feeling their strength. It was amazing what the able-bodied took for granted.

The same thought seemed to strike everyone at once, and the group fell silent.

"Come on, bro." Ted grinned at his brother. "I'll be the rock if you'll be the roll."

Danny laughed and swiveled his chair. "Just call me Arthur Murray on wheels."

Everybody laughed and the awkward silence was broken.

"So you'll come?" Ted asked eagerly.

Danny shook his head. "Nah, not tonight." He reached out and pulled Melissa into his lap. "We'd sort of planned on an intimate evening for two."

Melissa smiled tightly at the group. "You guys go on."

Lauren hoisted her backpack. "I'm up for it. But I want to go by my dorm first and change into some dry socks and boots. My feet have been wet all day."

"I want to go by my room too," Faith said, threading her arms into her yellow rain slicker. "I want to change into some jeans and get my bigger poncho."

Ted pulled something voluminous and made of waterproof canvas over his head. "Okay," he said. He took Faith's arm and began propelling her toward the door. "Last chance to change your mind," he called out to Danny.

"You guys have fun," Danny said, wrapping his arms tighter around Melissa.

There was a chorus of good-byes and a silly show of trading umbrellas as Dash, Lauren, Ted, and Faith made their way to the front door and prepared to brave the rain.

"See you guys at the dance," Dash said as he and Lauren hurried away, holding hands as they ran through the dark rainy night in the direction of Lauren's dorm.

"I hate going off and leaving Danny," Faith said as Ted pulled on her hand, leading her out into the downpour. "I feel like we should have tried harder to talk him into coming. I get the impression he's a little lonely sometimes."

Ted pulled a face. "You're right. But I think we have to respect his feelings and give him a little space. He'll get it worked out. Now, come on. Let's boogie so we don't feel like drowned rats at the dance."

Faith began to laugh and soon Danny was forgotten as she and Ted went stomping through deep puddles, comically zigging and zagging through others. Ted's warm hand felt good around her cold fingers.

"Hurry," Ted urged as they ran the last few feet toward her dorm with their heads lowered against the sheets of rain. The deluge was becoming more violent by the second.

They practically threw themselves inside the front doors of Faith's dorm and then leaned against each other for breath, laughing as the rain dripped off the ends of their noses.

Ted's blue eyes twinkled, and then stared seriously into hers for a moment. His gaze was so intense and so intimate that her breath caught in her chest.

Faith stared back, an echoing smile forming on her lips. They'd come a long way in a short time, she reflected. Ted wasn't the type of guy a girl could depend on. He'd made that clear from the beginning. So Faith had made up her mind not to depend on him. Not to expect anything from him. Ironically, the less she expected from him, the more he gave. It was as if he was growing up, and into a deeper and more mature relationship than either one of them had intended.

Ted lowered his eyes, breaking the moment. He dropped a kiss on the top of her damp head, then tugged on her hand. "Come on. Get changed and let's check out the dance."

Hand in hand they climbed the stairwell to the first floor. In spite of her wet clothes and dripping hair, Faith felt warm and secure. Happier than she had felt in weeks.

But when she opened her dorm door, her heart plummeted down into her stomach and all the warm and happy feelings began to dissipate.

She had company.

Sixteen-year-old Stephanie Dubronsky sat cross-legged on Faith's bed in a pair of baggy jeans and a sweatshirt. Her eyes were red from crying and she had a big wad of crumpled tissues in her hand. Stephanie's long blond hair was damp and flat against her head and she was shivering miserably.

"Stephanie!" Faith cried.

Behind her she heard Ted's breath whistling through his teeth as he let out an unhappy sigh.

"Liza let me in," Stephanie sniffled, referring to Faith's roommate. "She said I could wait for you in here while she was at the Bumbershoot Dance. I hope it's okay."

"Of course it's okay," Faith soothed, hurrying over to the bed. She sat down next to Stephanie and took her hand. "We're your friends. Right, Ted?"

Ted stood in the doorway, looking slightly annoyed and more than a little uncomfortable.

"Right, Ted?" Faith repeated, throwing him a warning look.

"Right," he echoed.

Stephanie was a high-school student who had spent some time on campus during a Big Sister/Little Sister program. She had gotten off to a bad start almost immediately—behaving like a conceited, predatory, teen sex queen. It had been all pose, but some of the guys had taken her seriously. The result was that she had been date-raped by a prominent student on campus—Christopher Hammond, a respected theater major and the president of the ODT fraternity.

Christopher had been arrested and there had been a lot of pressure on Stephanie to drop the charges. It had been Faith and Ted who had encouraged her to see the thing through. They had promised her that they would stick by her all the way and give her all the support she needed.

"I'm scared," Stephanie said in a choking voice. "My folks are coming back from Europe next Saturday. Every time I talk to my father on the phone, he keeps telling me not to worry—that as soon as he gets home he'll get to the bottom of this. What does that mean? I told them what happened. I told the police what happened. I told my school counselor what happened. What does my dad think he's going to do about it?"

"He's probably worried to death," Faith replied, patting her hand. "He and your mom are over there in Europe. Something awful happened to you while they were gone. They feel helpless, and it's just hard for them to accept. When you talk to them face to face it'll be different. You'll see."

Stephanie's face crumpled and the tears began

trickling down her cheeks. "You don't know my folks," she choked. "You just don't know my folks." Her head slumped down until her chin rested on her chest.

Faith's heart ached for Stephanie. And for all the other thousands of rape victims who weren't getting the support and understanding they needed.

"Ahem!" Ted coughed to get her attention, then jerked his head slightly toward the hall.

"Excuse me for a second, Stephie," Faith said softly. She stood and hurried out the door where Ted was waiting.

"This is the third time she's been here this week," he whispered.

"I know," Faith whispered back. "We're all she's got."

"We're not enough."

"What do you mean?"

"I mean neither one of us is a therapist or a rape counselor. Sure, we can hold her hand and pat her shoulder, but I don't know that we're really doing her that much good."

Faith sighed. "Maybe this will stop when her folks get home. In the meantime I think I've got to stick by her. You go on to the dance," she urged. "I'll stay here with Stephanie."

"No way," Ted protested. "We both told her we would be here for her. I won't go back on my promise. I'm here, and I'm staying."

*   *   *

"So go to the dance," Danny said impatiently, wheeling his chair across the room and staring out the window at the rain. "Who's stopping you?"

"You are," Melissa shot back. "I just don't understand why you refuse to go. Ted is your brother. Faith and Lauren are two of my closest friends. It would be fun."

Melissa ran her fingers through her short red hair. Annoyance and irritation were making her feel warm, and she wondered if the freckles were standing out across her nose and cheeks. She removed the jacket to her heavy sweat suit and leaned over to loosen the laces of the old athletic shoes she wore when the weather was horrible. She was at the U of S on a track scholarship, and she was just now getting back to her normal routine after injuring an Achilles tendon. She would have enjoyed the exercise and the movement of dancing after weeks of crutches and Ace bandages.

She and Danny were still in his dorm room, picking up some of the clutter that had been left after the study party. As usual, Danny had smiled and joked and acted as though he was fine when Ted and the others were here. But the minute the door had closed behind them, the darker side of Danny had emerged. The Danny who was angry at fate and bitterly regretted what he'd lost the night his speeding car had wrapped itself around a tree and severed his spinal cord.

Danny laughed dryly as he leaned over sideways to scoop a paper cup up off the floor. "You know, I do stoic real well." He balled the paper cup up in his hand. "And my other act, the cripple-with-the-great-sense-of-humor, goes over real good too. I smile, I tell jokes, I work out at the gym, and I go to class. But sometimes, Melissa," he said, the heavy irony in his voice turning to savage sarcasm, "I just don't *feel* like *dancing*!" He spat the last word as he flung the paper cup into the metal garbage can where it landed with a thunk.

Melissa sat down on the bed and sighed heavily, anger and pity warring in her breast. She didn't know what to say, didn't know what he wanted from her.

An argument? *How dare you sit there feeling sorry for yourself? You've still got more going for you than most people ever dream of.*

Agreement? *I don't blame you for feeling sorry for yourself. Believe me, if I were in a wheelchair I'd feel sorry for myself too.*

Melissa clenched her fist in frustration, feeling the nails dig into her palm. She had no idea what would make him feel better about himself, about his life, about his future.

Danny's face contorted and he took some deep breaths. He put his hands to his face, hiding it for a moment. When he removed them, the face was serene again. "I'm sorry," he whispered. "I don't know why I do this to you, of all people. I'm sorry. I'm sorry. I'm sorry." He held out his arms, and Melissa went over to him.

"It's okay," she whispered as his arms wrapped around her waist.

"No, it's not," he argued, leaning forward and resting his cheek against her chest. "I don't have any right to take my anger out on you. I should have hit the gym or grabbed a pen and a sketch pad and drawn it out of my system, instead of treating you to a tantrum."

Melissa smiled and stroked the top of his hair. Her eyes rested on the sketch pad that was always jammed in the backpack that was draped across the back of Danny's wheelchair. "May I take a look?" she said.

"Sure." Danny released her waist and swiveled his upper body around and grabbed the pad. "Welcome to Danny Markham's one-man show." He opened the pad, flipped through it, and held it up. "Ta da!"

Melissa began to giggle uncontrollably. It was a cartoon drawing of Dash and Lauren. And it was obviously based on the article they had written about their camping trip. The picture depicted caricatures of Dash and Lauren comically cowering and staring with horror at an unassuming chipmunk.

"Take a look at these," Danny said, flipping several pages ahead. "It's a new series." He smiled and held up the pad.

Melissa frowned, studying the busy cartoon with fascination. The characters were all in wheelchairs—strange wheelchairs equipped with battery packs, rocket jets, and overhead propellers. It was a futuristic world in which everyone was disabled, and their high-tech wheelchairs, prostheses, and walkers were completely individualized.

The people in the wheelchairs were recognizable types. The Big Man on Campus. The Absentminded Professor. The Campus Homecoming Queen. The Muscle-Bound Jock. The Yuppie. The Hippie.

Danny turned the pages, and Melissa saw a story emerge with each drawing, every line, every bold stroke of the pen. Every concept was pure Danny: funny, courageous, irreverent.

"It's called 'Wheelchairs in Outer Space,' " he said.

"Why didn't you show those to Dash and Lauren?" she breathed. "I'll bet the paper would love to run some."

Abruptly Danny's smile disappeared and he shut the pad. "No," he said in a definite voice.

"Why not?" Melissa demanded.

"What if people don't laugh?" He raised one rueful eyebrow. "Or what if they do? I would never know whether they were laughing at my work or laughing at me."

"Oh, knock it off," Melissa said impatiently. "Those drawings are hilarious and you know it."

Danny shook his head. "People pretend too much around the disabled. I don't want people pretending they think my work is funny because they're afraid of hurting my feelings. I don't want them pretending about anything. Let me see if I can explain this." He rubbed his hand over his chin as he carefully chose his words. "People don't know how to deal with a disabled person, so they like to act as if the disability isn't there. That's why I didn't want to go to the dance. People would want to pretend that it's normal for some guy in a wheelchair to be there. And it's not."

Melissa stamped her foot impatiently. "Get over yourself, Markham. What makes you think everyone at the dance is going to spend two seconds thinking about you one way or the other? They're there to have a good time, not think about you."

Danny began to chuckle.

Melissa grabbed the pad and threw it toward her pile of books. "Besides, half the guys at any dance spend the evening sitting around and refusing to dance. What makes you think you would even stand out?"

"Because I'm so good-looking." Danny grinned and leaned forward to put his hands around her waist. "Come here," he said softly.

"Only if you're planning to dance."

"Can't we dance here?"

Melissa smiled and began swaying back and forth, humming a slow romantic tune that they both liked. Danny pulled her down into his lap and began humming along. He put his hands to the wheels and began rocking back and forth to the music.

Melissa let her head fall back against Danny's shoulder and watched his beautiful profile as his blond-tipped eyelashes fluttered down.

The muscles of his throat moved slightly as he hummed, and outside, the gentle rain kept the rhythm.

Melissa snuggled deeper into Danny's shoulder. She was glad they hadn't gone to the dance. This was better. Lots better.

Three

Brooks took another bite of eggs and chewed slowly and thoughtfully. It was Thursday morning. Even though the rain had stopped for the moment, the sky outside was still gray and threatening. He stared around the crowded Dining Commons. It had been decorated for Bumbershoot. Dozens of colorful umbrellas hung from the ceiling, striking a cheerful note.

For the first time in weeks—months, actually—he was feeling calm and in control. After a long period of emotional turmoil, he felt like the old Brooks Baldwin. The Brooks Baldwin who knew right from wrong. The Brooks Baldwin who was loyal to his friends. The Brooks Baldwin who stood up for what he believed was the truth. The Brooks Baldwin who would never intentionally hurt a girl.

So far, his freshman year had been an emotional roller coaster. First Faith had broken up with him after they'd been together for years. She'd never really given him any satisfying explanation. It had left him completely and utterly confused. What had he done wrong?

Then he'd started dating Melissa. He'd been convinced that he was in love with her and had asked her to marry him. She'd agreed. But second thoughts had crept up on him. He lost his nerve at the last minute and humiliated her by leaving her standing at the altar.

It had been horrible for both of them. And it had left Brooks feeling guilty, fearful of getting involved again, and even more confused. Should he have gone ahead and married Melissa? Spared her the humiliation of being jilted even though he wasn't sure of his feelings? Or did he do the right thing by backing out?

He still didn't know.

He did know that he had hurt her, though. And it was hard to live with that.

Next Angela Beth had come along. And somehow she had convinced him to turn KC in to the phone company for long-distance fraud. After that, his guilt and confusion had reached critical mass. He had felt so overwhelmed on the day he walked into Mountain Supply, he had thought he might explode.

But now, after being forgiven by KC, he felt absolved. He had known KC for years. It was nice to think she was still his friend. That was important to him.

Angela Beth sat across the table. Her dark hair was pulled back in a ponytail that seemed to have a life of its own. It moved like a plume, punctuating Angela Beth's excited chatter.

Brooks was only half listening. She had been in a good mood when they'd started breakfast, but somehow she'd gotten started on the subject of the Tri Betas and her eyes were beginning to snap angrily.

Angela Beth's fingers adjusted the soft cowl neck of her red sweater. He loved that sweater on Angela Beth. He studied her face, struck again by her incredible beauty. The almond-shaped dark eyes. The perfect red mouth with its tiny beauty mark in the corner.

It was too bad she wasn't nicer, he reflected. It was strange being so crazy about a girl he didn't really like.

But he was crazy about her. Or crazy over her. Or else she made him crazy. He still couldn't believe he had let her talk him into turning KC over to the phone investigator.

From now on he didn't care what Angela Beth

did, said, threatened, or promised. He wasn't going to do her dirty work for her.

He picked up his rye toast and carefully spread the butter to the edges. His confession to KC had taken a huge weight off of his shoulders. The guilt that had been eating him alive was gone and it made him feel lighter, stronger, better able to stand up for himself with Angela Beth.

". . . and furthermore," Angela Beth was saying, "any sorority that would have somebody like KC Angeletti as a member has no business acting so holier than thou."

Brooks stopped buttering and pointed his knife at Angela Beth. "Lay off KC," he said levelly.

Angela Beth's dark eyes opened wide in offended surprise. "I beg your pardon?"

"KC is an old friend," Brooks said. "Last week when I bought you that equipment at Mountain Supply, I told her that I was the one who informed on her to the phone company. And you know what she said to me?"

Angela Beth stared, her little red mouth hanging open.

"Nothing," he said. "Not one word. Now, that's what I call incredibly gracious and—"

"Gracious!" Angela Beth exploded across the table.

Several people turned their heads toward their table. Angela Beth disbursed a few tight smiles, then turned her attention back to Brooks. "I would hardly call KC's behavior gracious," she hissed. "From what you've told me, she started the conversation by encouraging you to climb Talisman Rock, which is practically a death sentence this time of year."

"Angela Beth!"

"Then she talked you into buying a whole bunch of expensive equipment just so she could get a job."

Brooks wearily closed his eyes and wished he had never told Angela Beth about that. She had been thrilled with the equipment he had given her—until she found out that he'd bought it at KC's suggestion. He had thought she would find the story of KC's job audition funny.

Angela Beth hadn't thought it was funny at all. She had just seen it as proof of KC's dishonest nature. Ever since, she had been reading sinister motives into everything KC and the Tri Betas did.

"Look at her over there," Angela Beth commented in a voice dripping with contempt. She nodded her head and the ponytail bobbed indignantly. "Sitting there like butter wouldn't melt in her mouth. I wonder what she's plotting now."

Brooks looked over and saw KC sitting several tables away with Faith, Liza Ruff, and Kimberly Dayton.

He put his fork down with a clatter, feeling his calm composure slipping away. Why couldn't

Angela Beth just shut up? Why did she have to go on and on and on about this stuff?

"I can't believe you told her it was you that turned her in," Angela Beth went on. "That was so stupid. You might as well have told her it was me. Now she knows that the Gammas have her number, and we'll never catch her again."

"Relax, Angela Beth. Your name never came up. And what do you mean, *catch her*?" he demanded impatiently. "Why are you so determined to believe KC is some kind of criminal mastermind? It's nuts. KC just got fooled into thinking that a few free phone calls didn't matter in the big scheme of things. She wasn't alone. Lots of others on campus made the same mistake. And as for telling her, I had to tell her," he said, trying hard to keep a lid on his temper. "I couldn't live with myself anymore."

Angela Beth stabbed petulantly at her food with her fork. "Honestly, Brooks. Sometimes I just don't . . ." She broke off in surprise when KC suddenly materialized beside their table.

"I have something to say to you," KC told Brooks in an ominous tone. "And it's important."

Brooks started to stand, but KC put her hand on his shoulder and forced him back into his seat. "Sit!" she ordered.

"What in the—" Angela Beth began.

"Shut up," Brooks snapped at her. Then he looked up at KC. He'd seen KC in a lot of moods, but he'd never seen her looking as angry as she did now.

"I didn't say anything to you last week at Mountain Supply because I was too worried about getting that job. And besides, I was too stunned and too angry to find the words to tell you what a back-stabbing creep I think you are."

There was a little scream of indignation from Angela Beth, but KC ignored her.

Brooks felt the blood draining from his face. He thought KC had forgiven him, that he and KC were still friends. But the look in KC's eyes was far from forgiving. Her voice was rising now and ringing out through the Dining Commons.

"If anybody had tried to tell me that Brooks Baldwin, one of my oldest friends, would actually do something that low to me, I wouldn't have believed them," KC was saying loudly.

People were beginning to dart glances in their direction. It seemed to Brooks that he was surrounded by a sea of gawking faces.

"Why did you do it?" she demanded. "Why did you try to ruin my life?"

The room seemed to tilt slightly, and Brooks reached for the edge of the table to steady himself. He felt so strange, as if he was going to faint, or be sick.

He watched KC's face. He saw the teeth bared and the lips moving. But he couldn't make out the words anymore. All he heard was a wall of shrieking, accusatory sound; not one voice, but a chorus. The combined recriminatory anger of all the women he had intentionally or unintentionally betrayed, humiliated, disappointed, or goaded to anger. Faith, Melissa, Angela Beth. And now KC.

"I'm sorry," he gasped. His chest felt tight and constricted. He couldn't get enough air. "I'm sorry." He felt utterly ill. And utterly humiliated. Exposed as the craven, cowardly back-stabber he really was.

Somehow he managed to stand. After a few lurching steps, he plunged toward the door of the Dining Commons and broke into a run as soon as he was in the hallway.

He threw himself against the double glass doors that led to the outside and heard the glass panes rattle in their aluminum frames as they flew open.

Outside, he gulped in the air, trying desperately to calm the queasiness and guilt that were so gut wrenching, his insides were cramping. He doubled over, clutching at his stomach.

"Brooks. Brooks." A soft voice was repeating his name. "Brooks, look at me. Please." The voice was low and insistent. "Brooks," it murmured.

A soft hand caressed the back of his neck. "I told you what she was like," the voice whispered.

He could feel Angela Beth's presence beside him, smell the perfume she always wore, feel the tendrils of hair that tickled his cheek as she pulled him upright and pressed her face to his. "Stop it," he begged hoarsely.

"I can see you're upset. You shouldn't be. Don't ever let somebody like KC upset you. She's not worth it. Doesn't this show you that I've been right about her all along? She's poison. Please promise me you'll stay away from her."

Argh! She was at it again—on him about KC. It was like some kind of obsession with her. Brooks shook her hand off and began walking toward his dorm. "Leave me alone," he repeated.

"Where are you going?" Angela Beth demanded.

"I'm going climbing. I'm going to Talisman Rock."

"Talisman Rock! That's crazy. Why would you go up there now? Because KC suggested it?"

"No. Because I need to prove to myself that I still have some courage," he said wearily. "That I'm still a man and not the weak traitor you talked me into being."

Suddenly Angela Beth's arms were around him. "No," she breathed heavily into his ear.

"I need to be alone, Angela Beth." He reached up and tried to detach her arms from around his neck. "I need to be where it's just me and the mountain and the ice."

"Nobody needs to be alone," she argued. "Not when they're unhappy." Her eyes held his and he saw them soften and beckon. Her lips curved into a tender smile. "What if I apologized?" she teased in a throaty voice.

Something inside Brooks began to surrender. He couldn't fight this Angela Beth. Not the Angela Beth whose voice was low and soft and whose lips were cool and firm.

She held him tighter, and Brooks felt his heart begin to beat faster. Her sweater clung to every curve of her body, and the black leggings she wore beneath it made her legs look long and sexy.

Angela Beth giggled in his ear. "We'll go rock climbing together," she said. "We'll go later in the season. After the thaw. And I'll use my wonderful new equipment." She reached up and stroked the line of his jaw. "Deal?"

"Deal," Brooks croaked.

She pressed her lips to his, and soon Brooks was lost in her caresses. Her kisses always did that to him. But deep down, in his heart, he was afraid he had just made a deal with the devil.

Four

The Student Union was packed with people, and the noise of folk music, conversation, and laughter created a happy roar. KC and Winnie Gottlieb stared around them in surprise. The Bumbershoot activities committee had really outdone themselves. The cavernous and usually colorless lobby had been turned into a marketplace, complete with a series of festive stalls that could have been part of a town square in Spain, Nigeria, Switzerland, or southern France.

It was the night of the International Food Festival. The air was thick with the pungent smell of exotic spices. Colorful blankets, strange plants, and pieces of folk art decorated the stalls. From one end of the market to the other, the vivid Imari colors of the Far East blended with the ocher and brown earth tones of the Americas, weaving a tapestry of every conceivable hue and texture.

The food servers from the Bumbershoot committee wore costumes from every country, but their costumes bore no relation to the country of origin of the food.

To the right, a black guy in a mustard-colored dashiki and red fez used a long-handled spoon to ladle sauerkraut and knockwurst onto a paper plate. To the left, a Dutch-costumed girl in a starched white cap and wooden clogs served up big helpings of mu shu pork. There was no rhyme or reason to any of it, but that's what made it fun, silly, and zany. That's what made it Bumbershoot.

KC's mood had been gloomy after her blowup in the Dining Commons this morning, but the Food Festival was doing a good job of lifting her spirits. She grinned at Winnie, who fit right in. Her clothes were always fun, silly, and zany. Tonight she wore her customary spandex tights and Flintstones earrings. But in honor of the international theme, she had added a sombrero from Mexico, lederhosen from Germany, and a short, bright red, pink, and green kimono from Hong Kong.

KC watched Winnie tuck half of a croissant into the pocket of her leather lederhosen. She'd seen an amazing amount of food disappear into that pocket this evening. "Winnie," KC warned. "We're going to have mice if you don't stop this."

"It's just for a few more days," Winnie assured her. "My allowance will be here soon, and I'll get a nonresident Dining Commons pass. Unless I go completely nuts and invest the money in a phony gold mine or something. Or give it to a homeless person. Or blow it at the vintage clothing store. I'm having kind of a hard time acting like a grown-up these days."

Winnie scratched her forehead underneath her sombrero. "Wow. This straw stuff is itchy," she commented. She scratched again and pulled the hat down low over her eyebrows. "How's this? Think anybody will recognize me? I mean, if you were Josh and you saw me, would you think, 'Hey! There's Winnie and she looks awful and I'll bet it's because she's still in love with me and wishes she had me back'? Because I'd really hate that. I may not have a Dining Commons pass, but I still have some pride. Even though it's really hard to hang on to your pride after your husband falls for somebody else and doesn't even try to get in touch with you to see if you have any feelings left for him and. . . ."

A food server hurried past with a tray full of stuffed grape leaves. The passing food distracted Winnie's attention and momentarily stemmed her flow of chatter.

Winnie whisked one of the stuffed grape leaves from the tray with the deft hands of a pickpocket. From the depths of the lederhosen, she produced a Baggie. She dropped the stuffed grape leaf in, licked her fingers, and then secreted the Baggie somewhere in the kimono.

It was on the tip of KC's tongue to tell her in no uncertain terms that she had to quit bringing food back to the room, but she didn't have the heart to scold. Poor Winnie. Her gamine face was waiflike now. And she was looking more pathetic and wacked-out every day. There was just no way to beat up on her without feeling like a bully. Besides, letting Brooks have it had exhausted KC's energy for telling people off.

KC stuffed her hands down into the pockets of the long, navy-blue blazer she wore over her slim jeans and white cotton shirt, watching the crowd and listening with one ear while Winnie rambled on.

"I go to the Crisis Hotline, but I won't even answer the phones," Winnie said in a small voice. "Heck, who am I to give advice? I'm not exactly handling my own problems. I get my days mixed up. I show up at the wrong class at the wrong time. I . . ."

There was lots more. Nothing KC didn't already know. Winnie was losing it. She was definitely losing it. Losing it in KC's teeny, tiny, *single* study dorm room.

Between coping with Winnie, dealing with her

new job, and trying to come to grips with Brooks's perfidious betrayal, KC was getting close to losing it too.

KC looked around the crowded festival, hoping to catch sight of Faith. Maybe a talk with Faith would bring Winnie back to the planet surface. Come to think of it, a talk with Faith wouldn't hurt KC, either. Neither one of them had seen much of Faith in the last few days.

She caught sight of a familiar blond braid as the crowd parted slightly, and then her heart stopped. Beside Faith stood a tall, broad-shouldered guy in jeans, a denim shirt, and cowboy boots. His long, dark-brown hair hung down the middle of his back.

It was Cody.

KC hadn't spoken to him since the day he had told her good-bye. But maybe, just maybe, he was ready to bury the hatchet. And maybe, just maybe, he was ready to talk about getting back together.

". . . so anyway, all I can do about it is eat." Dimly KC became aware that the monologue that had been droning on in the background had come to an end. "Oh, look!" Winnie cried, clamping her hand down on her sombrero. "Hot dogs!"

Winnie tacked off toward a stall that was decorated like a baseball-stadium concession stand, and KC began drifting in Cody's direction.

As she drew closer, she saw that Melissa, Ted,

Dash, and Lauren were part of the group. Everyone was holding a paper plate heaped with exotic foods. They were all trying to talk, eat, and laugh at the same time.

". . . this Alice and Gustav Mulch, the Nature Twins . . ." Dash was saying, waving his fork in front of Cody. "These two are what? Completely dysfunctional? Riddled with unresolved sibling-rivalry issues? Co-dependent with trees?" He opened his arms and brought his shoulders almost up to his ears like a stand-up comic. "What's the motivation there, Cody?"

"That's up to y'all," Cody answered with a genial grin. "When I interview the Nature Twins, I want to be as surprised as my listeners at what Alice and Gustav have to say."

"Don't think just verbal," Ted said quickly to Dash and Lauren. "Think visual, too. I'm going to be videotaping the interview for my media class," he explained to Cody. "Which takes a little academic pressure off for the moment. One assignment *nailed*!" He gave a macho grunt and brandished his fist in a mock victory salute.

Faith stuffed a piece of sushi in her mouth. "I'm going to help with the videotaping. It's the least I can do for Ted since he helped me out on Waldo's film project," she said through her mouthful of rice.

A small piece of seaweed clung to the corner of Faith's mouth, and Ted wiped it with his napkin.

"I can't take her anywhere," he said.

The group laughed.

"And don't be fooled by this altruistic *least-she-can-do-for-me* routine," he teased. "Did she also mention that she would earn two credits for her popular-culture seminar?"

Cody threw back his head and laughed. "Are there any other angles I should know about?"

KC hovered at the perimeter of the laughing circle, waiting for an opportunity to join in the conversation and speak to Cody. But before she could say anything, Dash and Lauren began groaning histrionically.

"Videotaping this thing might take some of the pressure off you guys," Dash moaned. "But that's more pressure on us to come up with decent material. Now you're talking production values, costumes, lighting. Real jokes—not just funny accents."

Melissa took a bite of taco and quickly wiped her chin. "Why don't you ask Danny to write you some jokes?"

"Where is Danny, anyway?" Dash asked.

Who cares where Danny is? KC thought irritably. Cody hadn't even looked in her direction yet, and neither had anybody else.

Melissa chewed deliberately for a long moment. "He's at physical therapy," she answered finally and without inflection.

Just then Cody glanced her way. KC's heart

skipped a beat as his eyes rested for a moment on her face, then moved on. He leaned over and put his plate down on a nearby table stacked with dirty plates. "Don't get too freaked out," he said to Lauren and Dash. "It's supposed to be fun."

"Are you leaving?" Lauren cried.

"I've got to get to the station," Cody answered. He backed out of the circle and it immediately constricted again, leaving him outside the perimeter, facing KC. A slow, friendly smile creased his tanned face. "How are you, KC?"

He paused, waiting for an answer. But his body was poised to move on as if he weren't entirely sure she would want to talk to him.

"Fine," she said quickly. KC stepped closer to him, hoping he would read the body language correctly.

"Good," he said. "Well . . ." His smile began to look a little thin, and his mouth was white at the corners. "Have a good Bumbershoot," he said. He lifted his hand in a brief wave and took a step back.

KC took another step forward. "Listen, Cody, I couldn't help overhearing your conversation about the Nature Twins, and I was wondering if there might be some way I could get involved."

He reared back slightly, and his face took on an arrested look. "What was on your mind?"

Think, idiot. Think. The only thing that had been on her mind was starting a conversation with

Cody. Now she'd started it. And he'd put her on the spot. "Well," KC began, her mind racing as she improvised. "I was wondering whether there might not be some *commercial* application. Like, say . . . uh . . . for Mountain Supply," she added in a burst of inspiration. "Maybe Alice and Gustav could be the commercial spokespersons for Mountain Supply. The official *spokesfolks*," she suggested with a laugh.

Cody's eyes crinkled in an appreciative smile. "*Spokesfolks*. That's not bad."

Encouraged, KC plowed on. "Maybe Mountain Supply could lend Lauren and Dash some camping clothes and equipment to use as props and costumes. I'm working there now, you know." She dropped her voice. "To pay off the phone company."

Cody's slightly chilly demeanor warmed considerably. He reached out and squeezed her arm. "Good for you," he said sincerely. "That's great. I'm proud of you."

He twisted the silver bracelets he always wore in honor of his Native American heritage, and appeared to be thinking something through. After a long moment, he met KC's eyes squarely. "I'll come by Mountain Supply and talk to the owner. His name is Hindemann, right?"

"Right! That's great! I'll see you there."

Cody looked at his watch. "I've got to get moving," he said. "But I'll . . ."

She didn't want him to go. Reflexively, and without thinking, she reached out and caught his hand. The word "No" formed on her lips and then died as soon as she saw his startled look.

Immediately she dropped his hand and her cheeks colored hotly.

Cody seemed to understand. "It's good to see you too, KC," he said softly. "I think about you a lot. And I'm sorry about the way things ended. But I just couldn't go on after the way you treated me."

"I'm sorry," KC whispered in a strangled voice.

"I know," Cody said, letting his breath out slowly between his clenched front teeth. "But *sorry* is just a word. It's not a time machine. You're sorry, but it doesn't change anything that happened."

KC's eyes searched his face for some clue as to what he was feeling. What was the real emotion behind the words. Anger? Regret? Sadness? Was there any hope at all for reconciliation?

But the dark and impassive face revealed nothing. "I still want all the best for you," he said. "And I'd like us to be friends."

"Of course," KC agreed, forcing the lines of her face into a smile. "Of course we'll be friends."

"Good. That makes me real happy." He began to lift his hand again and then seemed to think better of it, thrusting it instead deep into the front pocket of his jeans. He backed up, smiling, then turned away, his tall frame moving easily into the crowd.

KC's eyes followed him until he disappeared in the sea of people.

"Don't do it to yourself," warned a voice at her elbow.

KC whirled around and saw Winnie eating a hot dog. The sombrero sat lopsided on her head, its chin strap dangling into her cup of soda.

"What are you talking about?" KC demanded irritably.

"I heard that conversation. And I know that look in your eye. I've seen it before—in the mirror. You're setting yourself up for disappointment. Take it from somebody who's been there."

KC pursed her lips. "You have to learn to read between the lines, Winnie. He thinks about me a lot. He wants the best for me. He wants to be friends. He—"

"Bingo!" Winnie shouted, cutting her off and stabbing the air with her hot dog for emphasis. "Cody is *Mr. Honesty*, right? He says what he means and he means what he says. If he says he wants to be friends, that means he wants to be *friends*. Period."

"Well, sure. That's all I want too," KC lied.

"Oh yeah, right," Winnie said sarcastically, pulling another Baggie from her pocket.

Suddenly KC was furious. Who did Winnie

think she was, anyway? Why was she projecting like this? Josh might be ready to call it quits with Winnie, but that didn't mean Cody was ready to call it quits with KC. At least not forever. There was hope. There was always hope. Where did Winnie get off raining on her parade like this?

KC snatched the Baggie from Winnie's hand and threw it into one of the tall garbage cans. "Stop it," she exploded. "You must have enough stuff in those pockets to last you a month. Why do you have to take some soggy old leftover hot dog home? Isn't my room a big enough mess already?"

"KC!" Winnie said, shocked. "Why are you always getting so mad at me?"

Melissa let herself into the room she shared with Lauren and flipped on the light. Lauren and Dash had said they wanted to hit another couple of stalls at the Food Festival before calling it quits. Melissa would have stayed with them, but she had at least another hour of studying to do before she went to bed. She was premed and that meant her academic schedule was incredibly demanding.

She crossed directly to her desk and began flipping through a tall stack of books and papers in search of her chemistry book. Where was it? She riffled through a second stack. The thick pile of books and papers had been sitting on her desk since the night of the study party in Danny's room.

Her fingers closed over the spiral binding of a drawing pad. Uh-oh. How did she get home with this?

Then she remembered snatching the pad out of Danny's hand and tossing it on the floor. She wondered if he had been looking for it. Probably not. Danny went through a pad a week sometimes. There were dozens of them scattered around his room and shoved under his bed.

She pulled the pad out of the stack and tossed it on Lauren's bed. She'd get it back to him tomorrow or the next day.

"Hi," Lauren said then, sticking her head around the door. "You still decent? Can Dash come in?"

"Sure." Melissa smiled. "Did you two finally get enough food?"

"Did we ever," Lauren said, coming in with Dash close on her heels.

Immediately Dash let out a groan and flopped across Lauren's bed. "Bring on the antacid pills, please."

Melissa smiled. "Too much food, I take it."

"Too much pressure," Dash corrected. "We saw Greg on the way out and he wants our next column yesterday. If Lauren and I don't come up with something brilliant, topical, and hilariously funny for the Bumbershoot supplement, our name is mud."

Lauren smiled. "Forget Alice and Gustav

Mulch jokes; maybe we could get Danny to write our next column for us. I wish he'd been at the festival. How come he has physical therapy at night?"

"He doesn't," Melissa said. "That's just what he wants me to tell people. He wasn't at physical therapy. He was in his room."

Lauren and Dash exchanged a look. "Alone?" Lauren asked softly.

Melissa paused. "Yeah. He's doing that a lot lately—really isolating himself. Every day he's less and less willing to get out, see people, do things. All he does is draw."

Dash whistled. "I'll say he draws. Look at this, Lauren."

Melissa's stomach clenched. Danny was almost fanatically private about showing his drawings to anyone but her. And now Dash was nonchalantly flipping through Danny's pad. He studied something for a long moment, let out a sharp crack of laughter, then flipped the page. He studied that page and laughed again. "These are great."

Lauren hurried to his side and sat down. Soon they were both laughing hysterically.

"These illustrations from our article are good," Dash said. "But these . . ." He held up the pad and tapped it with his finger. "These are wicked."

"The 'Wheelchairs in Outer Space' series?"

Dash nodded. "There's a real edge here. A kind of in-your-face humor. It's not everybody's cup of tea, but I think most people would appreciate the art even if they don't appreciate the humor."

He flipped a page and smiled approvingly. "Yeah. Oh, yeah. Danny's got it. I was joking before when I suggested that he write our next humor piece, but now I'm serious. No joke. These cartoons tell a story, have a point of view, and editorial content as well. On top of that, they're entertaining and thought-provoking. I'm going to talk to him about submitting these for publication in the Bumbershoot supplement."

"You'll be wasting your time," Melissa said regretfully.

"How do you know?"

"I asked him already."

Dash pulled his bandanna down farther over his forehead in frustration. "So that's that."

Lauren removed her wire-rim glasses and wearily polished them on the sleeve of her brushed-cotton shirt. "These reluctant-artist types," she said.

Melissa sat down in her desk chair. "What if . . ." she began cautiously.

Dash and Lauren sat forward. "What if . . ." they repeated.

"What if . . ." Melissa began again, ". . . you printed them without his permission?"

Dash and Lauren exchanged a look.

"It would be unethical," Lauren said.

"Unethical for whom?" Melissa asked.

Dash frowned. "What are you getting at?"

"Unethical for you to print them? Or unethical for me to give them to you?"

"Ah." Dash smiled slyly. "I see where you're going. You're wasting your time in premed, McDormand. You ought to be prelaw. That's very tricky reasoning."

Lauren looked confused. "Explanation, please."

"The cartoons are in my room," Melissa said. "In my possession. Possession is nine-tenths of the law. If I give you the drawings, and give you my permission to publish them, then it's kosher."

"It's not kosher," Lauren argued. "And it's not cricket, either."

"But it *is* legal," Dash said with a grin. "I say let's do it."

"The supplement goes to press right away. There would be no time to withdraw them if Danny freaked out," Lauren argued.

Melissa chewed on her bottom lip. Would he be furious? Maybe. But maybe he would be pleased. Pleased to know that somebody cared enough to push him a little.

It would be a real dose of shock therapy. And Danny needed shocking, something drastic to blast him out of his isolation.

"Let him freak out," Melissa said stubbornly. "He's had it coming to him for a long time."

Five

Winnie peeped out from under the blanket with one eye and watched KC tiptoe toward the door, slip out, and shut it quietly behind her.

Something about seeing KC up, fully dressed, and leaving for the Tri Beta house made Winnie feel even more depressed than she usually felt on a rainy Saturday afternoon. Once again, she had that everybody-has-a-purpose-in-life-but-me feeling.

She sat up and pushed aside the mountain of junk that always seemed to pile up over her sleeping bag in the night: her hot comb, some *True Romance* comic books, a Barbie doll with no head, and something green and fuzzy that might have started out as a breakfast pastry.

The rain was coming down in sheets, and a thick, heavy gloom descended around her as she surveyed her belongings. Hard to believe that these were the personal effects of a girl whose SAT scores had ranked her in the top-fifth percentile.

If I'm so smart, what am I doing sleeping all day on KC's floor with no place to go, nothing to eat, and nobody to talk to? Why am I sitting here feeling so overwhelmed by everything I need to do that I don't do anything?

There was a scuffling sound in the corner. Winnie frowned. Whatever was scuffling was squeaking now too.

Almost wincing with disgust, Winnie turned her head in the direction of the noise. She didn't want to see this. She really didn't. Maybe she was imagining things.

No such luck.

Over in the corner, a little gray mouse gave a half-eaten bag of taco chips an interested sniff.

"AIIIEEEEE!" Winnie shrieked, jumping to her feet and reaching for a weapon. Her hand closed over a folder, and she lobbed it toward the mouse. The folder bounced harmlessly off the wall over the mouse's head, but sent the creature scurrying toward the baseboard, where it disappeared into a tiny hole.

Winnie hurried over and began stuffing the hole with a pair of spandex tights. "I hate meeces to pieces," she muttered. Somewhere, she had read that you were supposed to use steel wool to plug a mousehole. Not having any steel wool, she looked around for the next-best thing and reached for another pair of spandex tights heavily shot through with metallic thread.

She stuffed them in, then reached for the folder and began to crumple it so that she could plug the hole. But she caught herself just in time. The folder was her Crisis Hotline Guidelines—the information she had been given when she first signed up to work as a Hotline counselor.

She hadn't spent much time at the Hotline recently. No productive time, anyway. Mostly when she went, she just complained about the doughnut selection and the lack of real cream for the coffee. It irritated her to death that they used those little packets of chemical whitener instead of cream or milk. No wonder she didn't go much anymore. She had too much respect for her health.

Give it up, Gottlieb. It doesn't get much lamer than that. Winnie went over to the mirror and picked up her comb, pulling it through the mats of her hair. She hadn't been to the Hotline because she'd been too busy feeling sorry for herself to worry about anybody else's problems.

That was dumb. One thing she'd learned at

the Hotline was that helping others was almost always a good way of helping oneself, too. During the time when Winnie had volunteered effectively there, her whole life had seemed to fall into place.

Now she was avoiding it, and along with it, avoiding all the problems that were bringing her down. Problemo numero uno being—no place to live.

She reached for an empty bag of junk food and balled it up. It was time to quit lying around feeling sorry for herself. It was time to start putting her life back together.

Winnie reached down and plunged her hand into the pile of clothes that had accumulated at the end of her sleeping bag. Black tights and a long gray sweater. Not very exciting. But businesslike. Winnie was ready to get down to business.

She rubbed her hand over the top of her head and checked the result in the mirror. A little flat. But today wasn't the day for spikes.

Winnie seated herself in KC's desk chair, grabbed a piece of paper, and quickly composed a "room wanted" ad. She would drop it off by the newspaper, then she would walk up and down the blocks that surrounded the campus and see if she saw any "room for rent" signs. After that, she would contact the housing office and put her name on a waiting list for a dorm room. That way she would have all the bases covered.

Three rewrites later, Winnie was finally satis-fied. She donned her rain slicker, waders, and fish-ing hat, and hurried out of the room with her spirits high for the first time in a very long time.

The hallways of Langston Hall seemed particu-larly gloomy today. The rain outside made the day almost as dark as evening, and the fluorescent lights flooded the hallway with a dim and jaun-diced light. Winnie's good spirits were rapidly waning with each step.

By the time she went downstairs and reached the lobby door, it was all she could do to keep putting one foot in front of the other. She shoved the door open and stepped outside onto the ce-ment porch.

It was as though she'd just given Mother Nature the signal she had been waiting for. The steady drizzle immediately turned into a violent downpour. The wind was blowing now, and the trees were bending and swaying. Winnie's fingers closed into balls inside her pockets. It wasn't fit for man nor beast out there.

Rain, rain, go away. On second thought, go ahead and rain. I'll come back another day.

Winnie trudged back in and up toward KC's room. It might be small, and it might be full of mice. But right now, it was home.

"Well, look who's here," an unpleasant voice commented in a sarcastic southern drawl. "What a surprise."

Winnie turned and saw Marielle Danner leaning against the open door of her dorm room, which was located across the hall from KC's.

Winnie smiled cautiously. Marielle could be nice occasionally. But most of the time, she was nasty. It had been Marielle who had tried to get KC blackballed from the Tri Beta sorority at the beginning of their freshman year. And it was Marielle who had gotten KC involved with drugs. KC had stopped doing drugs, but Marielle was still using and it showed.

Winnie stared in appalled fascination at the girl who had, a short time ago, seemed to have it all together—clothes, looks, and schoolwork. Now Marielle's sleek black hair hung in greasy strands around her shoulders, and her complexion was blemished and sickly. Marielle smiled crookedly. "It's Winnie Gottlieb, otherwise known as *The Best Friend Who Came to Dinner*."

"What does that mean?" Winnie asked warily.

"It means you showed up one night for a visit, and you've been here ever since." Marielle giggled. She took a drag of her cigarette and blew the smoke out through her nose. "Relax. I'm not the Dean of Women."

Winnie forced herself to smile. "It's just temporary," Winnie assured her. "I mean, I'm looking for a place of my own, and . . ."

Marielle's pencil-thin brow arched skeptically. "Whatever you say, sweetie. Listen, I didn't come out here to talk to you about your rooming situation." She coughed into her hand, a phlegmy-sounding smoker's cough. Then she smiled. "I thought you might want to join me in getting high."

Winnie took a step back. "I don't think so."

"You disappoint me. I thought you would jump at the opportunity. I mean, you look pretty hip."

"I just like to have fun with my clothes," Winnie said softly. Marielle's eyes were looking glassier by the minute. Whatever she was using was obviously kicking in.

Suddenly Marielle's benign demeanor vanished, and her lip curled in a pronounced sneer. *"I just like to have fun with my clothes,"* she mimicked in a whining falsetto.

Marielle took a menacing step closer to Winnie. "You know how I like to have fun? Ever see a cat with a mouse?" She swayed slightly. "Ever see the way it corners it, and then just tortures it with the suspense?"

Marielle burst into high-pitched hysterical laughter. "How about you be Jerry and I'll be Tom?"

Winnie's face frowned. Marielle was really out there.

"I'm not the Dean of Women," Marielle slurred again in a sinister tone, stepping closer and gripping Winnie's upper arm. "But I wonder what the Dean of Women would think about KC's illegal roommate. Don't you worry that some good citizen might just decide the housing office really should know about this little arrangement?" Marielle threw her head back and laughed hysterically.

Frightened, Winnie wrenched her arm from Marielle's grasp and ran back toward the staircase with tears streaming down her face. This was horrible. The last thing in the world she wanted to do was get KC into trouble.

Rain or no rain, Winnie plunged into the bleak afternoon weather. She had to talk to somebody. And Faith was the best listener she knew.

Angela Beth sat on the overstuffed chintz sofa next to her best friend, Christine Van Diem. Several of the girls had met at the Gamma house for a cleaning session, and now they were taking a break from waxing and sweeping so they could gossip.

Her long red nails snapped and fidgeted as she listened to Christine and some of the other Gammas discuss the biggest scandal to hit Greek Row all year—the arrest of Christopher Hammond for the alleged date rape of Stephanie Dubronsky.

"I just don't understand what a high-school girl was doing at a college frat party in the first place," a tall blonde in a short skirt and sweater said disdainfully. "She must have been wearing something incredibly provocative."

"Oh, come on," another girl argued, her voice strident with anger. "Women aren't responsible for men's sexual behavior. No guy has a right to rape a girl just because she's dressed provocatively, because she lets him kiss her, or any other reason they may claim. They control themselves at the beach, so why don't we expect them to control themselves at a party?"

"That's true," another girl said, nodding. "I agree one hundred percent. Christopher Hammond ought to go to jail if he's guilty."

"If anybody ought to go to jail, it's that girl's parents," the tall blonde said with a sniff. "If they'd been on the ball, that girl wouldn't have been at a frat party with guys who were too old, too drunk, and too wild for her to handle."

Angela Beth's fingernails pressed together so hard that one of them broke off. Who cared about Christopher Hammond or Stephanie Dubronsky? As far as Angela Beth was concerned, they were both scum. Neither one of them was worth the wedge that was being driven through the campus, and through the sorority and fraternity houses.

The sound of several voices arguing at once made her so irritable, she couldn't stand it anymore. "Oh, what difference does it make if he's guilty or not?" she exploded, jumping to her feet. "Don't any of you realize how divisive this is turning out to be? How bad this makes the ODTs look? How bad it makes the Gammas look? How bad it makes the whole Greek system look?"

"What are you saying?" Christine cried. "That we should all just sweep it under the carpet so we don't have to argue about it?"

There was a burst of volatile emotion and within moments, Sally Truman, the president of the Gammas, came charging out of the house office with the sorority accounts book in her hand. "What's going on out here?" she demanded.

"We were discussing the Christopher Hammond mess," someone answered in a low voice.

The pledges fell silent, and some girls exchanged hurt and angry glances.

Sally put her hands on her hips. "Look. We've all got to keep a grip. This is the kind of thing that pushes everybody's buttons and gets people excited. But all this screaming and yelling is a waste of time. Nobody knows for certain what happened that night except Stephanie Dubronsky and Christopher Hammond. If anybody's got information—saw anything, heard anything—that would either implicate or clear Christopher, they need to speak up to the authorities. Otherwise . . . the best thing we can do is stay calm and not get all bent out of shape before the case even gets to trial."

"But Sally . . ." one of the girls began.

There were more passionate arguments presented for either side, but Angela Beth was only half listening. She was so angry, so enraged, that her hands were actually shaking. Was she the only one who saw the truth? The only one who saw that this whole thing was the fault of that Faith Crowley, and by extension, KC Angeletti and the Tri Betas?

They were like some troika from hell. They were ruining her life. Everything Angela Beth did, or reached for, they managed to somehow spoil. She had lost her job in the biology lab when Faith Crowley and her artsy friends had raided the place and ruined a series of important experiments. That lab had been under Angela Beth's supervision, and her academic supervisor had unfairly held her responsible.

Then, in spite of all her hard work and effort to make the Gammas the top sorority, the Tri Betas had beat them by raising the most money in the All-Sorority charity auction.

It should never have happened that way. Angela Beth had convinced Brooks to inform on KC to the phone company. He'd done it, and Angela Beth had fully expected KC to be arrested at the auction, and the Tri Betas to be demoralized and discredited. But somehow KC had eluded arrest and worked out some kind of deal. The Tri Betas had emerged from the messy phone scam not only unscathed, but more firmly on top than ever.

And now, to top it all off, Faith Crowley had somehow thrust herself into the middle of the

Christopher/Stephanie fracas, urging the stupid girl to press charges and prolonging the whole horrible ordeal.

If only she could turn the tables on them all. Her mind began racing and planning. There had to be a way. There just had to be. It would be nice to see KC lose her job, for one. That would show her.

And if only there were some way to clear Christopher Hammond. Faith Crowley would look like a fool if he was exonerated. And so would that boyfriend of hers.

". . . so let's remember that we're all Gammas . . ."

A comradely arm draped over Angela Beth's shoulder, bringing her thoughts back to the present.

The arm belonged to Sally, and from the sweet, singsong sound of her voice, she was just wrapping up the we're-sisters-so-let's-all-be-friends speech.

Well, that was fine. The Gammas *were* her friends.

But KC wasn't. And neither was Faith.

They were her enemies. They'd caused a lot of trouble for her. And they were going to have to pay.

As soon as the car began to slow for the stoplight, Stephanie reached for the handle of the door. "I will not go back to the police and say it didn't happen!" she shrieked. *"I won't, and you can't make me."*

The car came to a stop and Stephanie jumped out, stumbling in her haste. "Stephanie!" she heard her father shout angrily as she slammed the door shut.

Stephanie began to run. Behind her, she heard her parents' car doors open. "Stephanie!" her mother yelled. "Please come back!"

Stephanie threw a look over her shoulder and saw both her mother and father standing in the middle of the street beside their parked car. Vehicles behind theirs were now stuck in a long line. Curious faces watched her from car windows as she ran by them in her blue jeans, pullover sweater, and running shoes.

"Stephanie, come back!" she heard her father yell. It sounded like an order this time. "We have to talk about this."

"Please don't run off!" Her mother's voice sounded high and thin.

Stephanie turned her head and caught one last glimpse of her mother's shocked face and her father's angry scowl through the blur of her tears. Then she veered between the cars, heading toward the U of S campus. Fortunately the rain had let up for the present.

Stephanie kept running. "I knew they were going to do this," she choked. "I knew it."

She had driven her parents' car out to the airport to pick them up. As soon as she saw their faces at the gate, she knew there was going to be trouble. They had started in on her the second they cleared customs.

Veering onto the southern corner of the campus, she ran behind a high hedge as her stomach began to heave. Just thinking about the last two hours made her want to vomit. Her parents were impossible—sympathetic one minute, angry the next. Screaming at her. Screaming at each other.

It was *her* fault.

It was *his* fault.

No, it was *their* fault.

The upshot was they just wanted her to tell the police to forget it. "We're just thinking of you, honey," her mother had said in that quavery whine that Stephanie detested. "These things rarely result in a conviction, and almost always follow the girl for the rest of her life."

Stephanie retched into the flower bed, then sank down and wiped her sleeve across her mouth and nose. Was her mother right? Was it going to follow her all her life? Were people going to treat her differently forever?

As horrible as it seemed, maybe her parents were right. She didn't want people treating her like some kind of victim from now on. Or like some kind of whore.

Maybe she *was* a slut. Maybe it really *had* been her fault.

Her feet were moving now in the direction of Coleridge Hall. Talking to Faith had become a habit. But she almost wished she had somebody else to talk to when she was feeling this confused. Faith couldn't help her sort out the jumble of feelings. Neither could Ted.

They were all she had, though. She didn't have any friends in her high school. She had acted too stuck up for too long, and nobody there liked her. And the teachers were grown-ups. They were so busy getting upset over what had happened, they forgot to listen to her when she talked.

There was nobody in the lobby of Faith's dorm when Stephanie entered. She went up the stairwell to the first floor and was walking down the hall toward Faith's room when she saw a familiar girl coming toward her. It was Winnie. Winnie Gottlieb. Or Gaffey. Or something like that.

Sheesh! Was she weird! Stephanie's swollen eyes took in the poncho, the fishing hat covered with flies, and the waders. She looked just like her dad looked when he went fly-fishing. All she needed was a reel.

Winnie was staring at her, too. "I can tell by the red eyes and swollen nose that you're looking for Faith," Winnie said as the two girls met in the hall. She reached up and adjusted her hat. "Unfortunately she's not home, and neither is Liza. They're painting scenery in the theater department. And no, I don't know this because I'm psychic. I know it because Faith left a note on her door."

Stephanie felt her face fall. She had been counting on talking to Faith. Maybe even spending the night in her room.

Winnie reached into her pocket and pulled out a box of mints. "Want one?" she asked, holding out the box.

Stephanie shook her head. "No, thanks."

"Oh, go on," Winnie urged. "Take one. Take. Take."

It seemed important to her, so Stephanie reached into the box and popped the mint she took into her mouth. She smiled. "Thanks."

Winnie rattled the box and poured one into her own palm. She threw it in the air, bent back her head, and caught it in her mouth. "Good," she said, biting down on the mint with her front teeth. "Now that we've broken bread together, or eaten mints together, that makes us friends." She shot Stephanie a frank look. "So now you don't have to feel embarrassed about my knowing your situation. Okay?"

"I guess," Stephanie answered uncertainly.

"Fine," Winnie said agreeably. "You don't have to make up your mind about how you feel right now. You can think on it or sleep on it. That's what I tell people at the Hotline, anyway."

"The Hotline?"

"The Crisis Hotline. I'm a counselor. Though

you're probably wondering what a basket case like me could possibly tell someone who's having problems." Winnie lifted her fishing hat, spiked up her hair, and then squashed the hat back down. "Well, I don't have anything to tell them. Which is why I don't pick up the phone when I go there these days. So if you should call sometime, don't ask for me."

"Okay," Stephanie answered again. She couldn't tell if Winnie was serious or joking.

Winnie jerked her thumb over her shoulder in the direction of Faith's door. "Now, there's a girl who ought to have her own hotline. Right? Here we are, two of Faith's little lost lambs, wandering around with confused looks on our faces because we can't talk to Mama Faith. What do you think this says about us?" Winnie asked, popping a mint in her mouth. "I mean, what keeps us from calling our real mothers? Mine's a shrink, by the way. What about you?"

Winnie's question came so suddenly and abruptly, Stephanie was caught off guard. "What about me?" she asked carefully. She was having a hard time keeping up with Winnie's conversation.

"Is your mom a shrink?" Winnie asked.

"Oh!" Stephanie shook her head. "No."

Winnie shrugged. "That's too bad. You could probably use one. No offense intended." She smiled. "I'm going to drown my sorrows—literally—with a walk in the rain," she added. "I hope it's started up again. Care to join me?"

Stephanie was tempted. Winnie was frank and sort of funny, and in spite of her claims about being a basket case, she made Stephanie feel better.

But at the same time, Stephanie didn't know her that well. She wasn't sure how comfortable she felt with her. "No, thanks," she said shyly. "I think I'll wait for the rain to stop. Then I'll go over to Ted's."

"Okey-dokey," Winnie said. "Take care. Bye."

"Bye." Stephanie watched Winnie head down the hall and disappear into the stairwell. Then she leaned back against the hall wall, suddenly depressed again. Ted was a great guy. And Faith was a great girl. They were the two most wonderful people Stephanie had ever met.

So why did she feel so lonely when she was with them?

Six

Danny spun across the court, wheeled up behind Ted as he dribbled, and then leaned out, digging his elbow into the back of Ted's knee. Ted's leg collapsed and he began to fall. Startled, he let go of the ball. Danny took advantage of the moment. He grabbed the ball, put it in his lap, and began quickly rolling his wheelchair away.

"Foul!" Ted yelled.

"So what?" Danny shouted gleefully. He dribbled the basketball from the side of his wheelchair and eyed the basket, his mind calibrating the distance, the speed, and the trajectory. He shot. "All right!" he screamed as the basketball fell through the hoop with a loud clattering sound that reverberated throughout the empty gym.

It was Sunday night, and the two brothers had gotten together for a little one-on-one. Danny swiveled the chair one hundred and eighty degrees and gave Ted his cockiest grin. "Aren't you ashamed of yourself—falling for an old trick like that and getting beat by a cripple?" His face was wet with sweat, and the terry-cloth bands that he wore around his forehead and wrists were soaked with perspiration.

Ted's dark-green T-shirt was drenched, and his hair was soaked. It had been a hard game.

The two brothers had always been competitive—grades, girls, games. It didn't matter. They fought for the prize, tooth and toenail.

"That wasn't fair," Ted said. He wiped his face against the shoulder of his T-shirt.

Danny picked up the ball and set it spinning on the tip of his finger. "Life's not fair. Why should basketball be any different?" He dropped the ball and sent it rolling across the shiny floor in Ted's direction. "But we can do it over if you want."

Two guys had just come into the gym and stood on the sidelines, waiting for the court. Ted picked up the ball and popped it back to Danny. "No time. This game's yours." He walked over to where they had left their gear. "But next time . . ." he wagged his finger and warned.

Danny nodded hello to one of the guys on the sidelines and flipped the ball in his direction. "We're done."

The guy caught it easily and grinned his thanks.

Ted tossed a towel toward Danny and grabbed both gym bags. He plopped one down in Danny's lap, then wordlessly headed for the side door where the wheelchair ramp was located. Danny wheeled after him.

Soon they were outside. There was no rain, but it was misting. Ted hadn't said a word since leaving the gym. His normally genial face was creased and there was a distinct furrow over his eyebrows.

"Hey," Danny said. "If you're that bent out of shape, I concede the game."

Ted shot him a surprised look. "Huh?"

"I thought I was being funny," Danny explained. "I mean, a dirty trick here and there is what used to make a game interesting. But I can tell by your face that you're peeved. So . . . I'm sorry. The game's yours."

Ted broke into a grin and began to laugh. "I wasn't thinking about the game, you goofball. I was thinking about Faith."

"You always look that serious when you think about Faith?" Danny smiled and turned his face up to the sky, enjoying the sensation of the cool mist collecting on his forehead and cheeks. "Boy, things have really changed, haven't they?" He lowered his head and stared quizzically at Ted. "I never thought I'd see you frowning and worrying about a girl. Always more where the last one came from, was your motto."

"Look who's talking," Ted countered. "You were always as bad as I was. I remember the night you had three dates—one at six, one at nine, and one for the midnight movie."

"Those days are over." Danny sighed. "And you know what? I'm glad. At least I think I'm glad. Life seems better somehow with just one girl."

"Same here," Ted agreed. "I can't imagine wanting to be with anyone besides Faith right now. For the first time in my life, the word *commitment* doesn't make me break out in a cold sweat."

"So why the big frown?"

Ted blew out his breath. "I'm ready for commitment. I'm just not ready for parenthood."

Danny's heart skipped a beat and he came to a stop so suddenly, he half expected the wheels on his chair to squeal. "Did you say *parenthood*?"

Ted lifted his hands, palms out. "Hold it, hold it. You're jumping to conclusions. I'm not talking about Faith and me having a baby. I'm talking about Stephanie."

Danny shook his head. "Now I'm really confused."

Ted laughed. "I'm not explaining this very

well. What I'm trying to say is that Stephanie spends almost every evening with me and Faith. It's like having a foster kid or something. Yesterday Faith was painting scenery at the theater, so Stephanie came over to my room until she got home. Then she was over at Faith's until one A.M."

"Ohhhh," Danny said. "I'm beginning to get it."

"Don't get me wrong. I know Stephanie needs friends right now—support, understanding, all that stuff. But I'm not sure she should be depending on Faith for so much of it."

"What about her parents?"

"They're trying to talk her into dropping the charges."

"You're kidding."

Ted shook his head. "No. And you can't blame them. They don't want to see her get hurt. If it goes to trial, she could get dragged through the mud. Let's face it. Their priority is protecting Stephanie, not punishing Christopher Hammond."

"What do you think she should do?"

Ted licked his lips. "Look. It doesn't matter what I think. Or what Faith thinks. Or what her parents think. Stephanie needs to get straight on what *she* thinks. And I'm not sure we're the best people to advise her."

"What does Faith say about all this?"

"That's the problem. I'm afraid if I say this to Faith, she'll just think I'm insensitive or emotionally unavailable. Or whatever it is that women say when they're trying to tell you you're a selfish heel. And I guess I am being selfish, because what's really worrying me is that this thing is going to come between me and Faith. We can't have a relationship with Stephanie sitting between us all the time." He scratched his chin and pushed out his cheek with his tongue as if he didn't like what he was going to say next. "And then," he said in a subdued voice, "I start thinking . . . so it doesn't work out. Big deal. The world is full of women, and . . ." He trailed off and shrugged his shoulders.

He didn't have to finish his sentence. Danny knew exactly how Ted felt. He had felt that way himself a hundred times during the course of his relationship with Melissa. The only difference was that Ted could probably break up with Faith at six and have a new girl lined up by seven.

Danny didn't think he had that option. The way he saw it, guys in wheelchairs didn't have the same appeal to women as guys on two healthy legs. He tried hard not to be bitter about it. And never, ever, to make Melissa feel as though he had *settled* for her because she was all he could get. He was crazy about Melissa.

"Well?" Ted said. "Does that silence mean you think I'm a jerk?"

Danny shook his head. "No. It just means I'm thinking. Thinking about relationships. Thinking about Melissa."

"She's a great girl," Ted said.

"I know she is. So why do I make life so hard on her?"

"I didn't know you did."

"I'm not proud of it. But I do. For some reason, the person I care the most about is the person I take out all my frustrations and anger on. It doesn't mean I'm frustrated or angry with her. But that's the way it keeps coming out."

"She understands," Ted assured him.

"Nobody understands," Danny said quietly. "They couldn't. Nobody could know what it's like to go to sleep at night and dream you're whole again. I dream about running. I'm always running in my dreams. And I can feel the blood and the bone and the muscle in my legs. There's a sense of joy. Euphoria. Like I've just discovered the meaning of the universe or something."

Ted swallowed, his eyes on Danny's face.

"Then I wake up and . . ." Danny slapped his hands against his lifeless thighs. "This is what I am. Half a man. And I have to get used to it all over again. Every single morning."

There was a long silence, and Danny felt a blush creeping up his neck. What had made him confide so much? He sounded like a wimp or something. Ted had his own problems.

"You're right," Ted said quietly. "Nobody could understand. I'm sorry you go through that. I'm glad you told me."

Danny shot him a look. Was he serious? Was he being facetious? He let out an embarrassed laugh. "Listen to us."

"Yeah, listen to us. We're talking. Maybe these relationships are teaching us something after all." He nodded toward the snack bar. It stayed open late and was located in a low building not far from the athletic complex. "Let's get something to eat before we head back to the dorms. We can keep talking."

"Okay by me," Danny agreed, turning the chair and rolling along behind Ted.

As they entered, they passed a stack of newspapers placed between the door and the pay phone. Ted reached toward the stack and grabbed one. "Here's the Bumbershoot supplement. Let's see what the lineup is for the next few days." He lifted the paper.

Danny listened to the music of the jukebox inside the snack bar and stared idly at the little squiggly drawings on the back of the newspaper Ted was reading. Strange. They reminded him of something.

He turned his head toward the open door of the snack bar and his eyes flickered over the crowd at the tables, his mind wandering for a moment. Then suddenly it hit him.

"What the . . ." he yelled, snatching the paper from Ted's hand.

"Hey!" Ted protested.

But Danny was already flipping the page. No wonder the drawings looked familiar. They were *his*. "Wheelchairs in Outer Space" was splashed across two pages.

Quickly, furtively, he shoved the newspaper into the bag on his lap. Then he grabbed several more and stuffed them in as well.

"What are you doing?" Ted demanded, looking at him as if he were crazy.

"Here," Danny said, picking up the last few supplements. "Take these over to the Dumpster behind the athletic complex and get rid of them."

"Why?"

But Danny was already rolling out the door. "Just get rid of them," he yelled over his shoulder. "I'll explain later."

How had his drawings—cartoons that reflected his most private thoughts and feelings about being in a wheelchair—wound up splashed across the newspaper? With his name on them, no less. It was nuts. It was a nightmare.

And somehow, he felt sure that Melissa was behind it.

As he crossed the campus, his heart was racing and he felt like a convict on the lam. Two good-looking girls gave him a long look from the other side of the dorm green and Danny wished he could just disappear. Every eye that turned in his direction seemed to be identifying him as the creator of the grotesque travelog called "Wheelchairs in Outer Space."

"Does that guy really think this stuff is funny?" he imagined their voices asking. Voices heavy with disbelief and contempt.

Soon he was wheeling up the ramp that led to Melissa's dorm. He was soaking wet. He stank. He was close to tears. This was the worst thing that had ever happened to him in his whole life. His eyes dropped to his legs for a second. The second-worst thing, he mentally amended.

He punched the elevator button and wheeled himself on and off with fury.

It was all he could do to knock instead of putting his fist right through Melissa's door.

Inside the room, he heard footsteps. The door opened and Melissa's curious face peered out and then smiled. "Danny!"

Danny reached into his bag, shook out the crumpled paper, and held it up. "Know anything about this?"

Melissa's face paled and her freckles stood out. "I take it you're not pleased."

"*Not pleased* doesn't even begin to cover it," he said through gritted teeth.

Melissa lifted her chin. "Sorry about that. I guess I goofed," she said lightly. She was trying to make her voice sound flip, trying to bluff her way through it with bravado. But Danny heard the little quiver in her voice that told him she knew it was a big deal. A very big deal.

"How dare you?" he demanded.

Immediately she dropped the act and reached out toward him. "Danny, I'm sorry," she said in a rush. "I thought it would be good for you, and . . ."

Danny backed up. "Don't touch me," he hissed.

Melissa drew back.

"You listen to me, and you listen good," Danny snapped. "Because I'm going to have this conversation with you exactly once. If we have it again, this relationship is *over*! I may be in a wheelchair, but that doesn't mean my brain doesn't operate. I'm capable of making my own decisions. I *don't* want you making them for me. I *don't* want you deciding what's good for me and what's not good for me."

He held the paper and balled it up. "You've made a fool out of me. I feel exposed. I feel humiliated. Do you think *that's* good for me?"

Melissa moaned slightly. "Please, don't. I'm sorry. I'm really, really sorry."

Danny's lips were shaking, he was so angry. It was all he could do not to burst into hysterical tears. He turned the wheelchair and started down the hall.

"Danny! Come back!" he heard Melissa call.

But he didn't stop. All he wanted to do was get back to his room.

And hide.

Seven

On Monday afternoon, KC worked her way up aisle seven of Mountain Supply, her sharp eyes keeping a lookout for items that needed restocking or shelf areas that needed neatening. Three boxed thermos kits were stacked upside down and KC quickly corrected that.

She was tired after a full day of classes, but she knew from experience that the best way for her to fight fatigue was to keep moving and busy.

It kept her in good with Mr. Hindemann too. He was turning out to be just as difficult as everybody said he was—bad tempered, demanding, extremely suspicious. He was always sure that everybody in the store—customers and employees alike—were just waiting for an opportunity to steal from him.

Her eyes swept the large store, looking for something to do. Things really were slow during the rainy season, and Mr. Hindemann leaned against his cash register, looking bored and irritable. They were the only people in the store.

Two faces suddenly appeared in front of the big display window on the street and peered in.

Mr. Hindemann perked up, eager for them to enter. But the two faces disappeared and the couple crossed the street without a backward look.

Mr. Hindemann sighed heavily. KC didn't blame the couple. She didn't know much about camping equipment, but she did have enough innate taste and merchandising sense to know that the display window didn't have much appeal.

"Mr. Hindemann," she began, trying to make her voice sound nonjudgmental. "I wonder if the display window is . . . well . . . as *compelling* as it could be."

"What are you getting at?"

"If I were arranging that display, I would put a red lantern on the table, and a bowl of colorful wax fruit. I'd put one of those really bright flannel shirts on the mannequin. Or better yet, I'd put one on the big stuffed bear. That would really grab people's attention and showcase the merchandise."

"I don't know," Mr. Hindemann said. "We're a serious sporting-goods store. That might look frivolous to serious outdoor types." He stroked his beard. "On the other hand, nobody's beating down the door to get in here. You could try it, I guess. But if anybody says it looks dumb, you have to change it back."

"Great," KC said with a grin. She grabbed an extra-large yellow and pink flannel shirt off the shelf and headed for the window. This would be fun, and it would keep her busy until quitting time.

She hoisted herself up into the display window and looked out onto the street. As usual, the sky was gray and dark, but it wasn't raining right now. She began to fit the flannel shirt over the out-stretched arms of the big bear that was the store's mascot and trademark. Then she saw two familiar faces coming out of the bookshop across the street.

Brooks and Angela Beth.

They were headed her way.

KC shrank behind the bear, trying to stay out of sight and pretend that she hadn't seen them. She could feel her temper rising. Her heart was beating faster, and her breath was coming a little more rapidly. She hoped they wouldn't come into the store, but they did. If Brooks said anything to her, KC knew she would probably start yelling. She concentrated on what she was doing. Still, she couldn't resist sneaking a peek. She looked over her shoulder toward the interior of the store. Her jaw dropped in outrage. Brooks had walked right up to Mr. Hindemann, and now the two of them were deep in conversation and glancing at her.

Brooks pointed in her direction, then turned back to Hindemann. Hindemann frowned, darted a look at her from beneath his heavy brows, then dropped his eyes to the floor, nodding his head as he listened intently to Brooks.

KC stepped out of the window to retrieve a display item and discovered herself face to face with Angela Beth. Angela Beth's eyes glinted dangerously. "I understand I have you to thank for my new climbing equipment," she said in a clipped voice. "I'm glad to have it," she continued before KC could respond. "A climber with my skills should have first-class tools. But next time, KC, I'd appreciate it if you would keep your gift ideas to yourself. I'd also appreciate it if you would refrain from making suggestions to Brooks about climbing sites."

KC looked toward the cash register. Hindemann was pointing at her now. Brooks was nodding.

". . . can't believe . . . iciest climb in the state . . . irresponsible . . . shouldn't be working here if you don't know better than to . . ."

Angela Beth's nasty voice was like the annoying buzz of an insect. KC was doing her best to ignore it. She was too busy keeping an eye on Brooks and Hindemann. They had finished their conversation and Brooks had wandered off. Hindemann was watching KC now. Or, more accurately, glowering at her.

". . . telling somebody to climb Talisman Rock is just stupid," Angela Beth finished irately. With that, she turned on her heel and stalked off to find Brooks, her ponytail swinging from side to side in righteous indignation.

Mr. Hindemann crooked his finger at KC. "KC! May I talk to you *privately?*"

KC's heart sank down into her stomach. Obviously Brooks had told Mr. Hindemann why she had been so desperate for this job. He knew she had stolen from the phone company.

No one has ever been given any reason to distrust KC Angeletti, she had told him.

It had been a lie. And Brooks had seen to it that Mr. Hindemann knew it. What was his problem? Why was he so determined to ruin her life? She was almost weeping with fury as she approached Mr. Hindemann. It was all so unfair. What had she ever done to Brooks that would make him so bound and determined to destroy her?

Ding! went the bell on the door.

Hindemann's eyes darted toward the door and lit up. "May I help you?" he asked.

KC turned to see Angela Beth and Brooks slip-

ping out the door as Cody and two of his friends
and cohorts from the radio station walked in.

Cody smiled at KC. "Hi, KC." Then he
bobbed his head at Hindemann. "Howdy."

"Take care of these people," Hindemann said
quickly to KC. "You and I will talk later."

Mr. Hindemann began to retreat to the back
of the store. KC gaped at Cody. She was completely at a loss. She knew she had talked to Cody
about something, but her mind was so full of
Brooks and the phone company and getting fired
that she couldn't focus. She couldn't for the life
of her remember what they had discussed, or why
Cody had come by.

Cody seemed to read her mind. "Excuse me,"
he said to Hindemann. "But we'd like to talk to
you *and* KC." He extended his hand toward the
returning store owner. "I'm Cody Wainwright,
the DJ at KRUS, the U of S station."

"Oh, right. I've heard your show."

Cody gestured toward his friends. "This is Joel
Albrecht, the KRUS station manager. And Dahlia
Drew, who does the news breaks."

Joel Albrecht was a baby media executive with
crisp jeans, a crisp white shirt, crisp hair, a flow-
ered tie, and a firm handshake. He nodded briskly
and gave Mr. Hindemann a crisp "How do you
do, sir?"

Dahlia Drew was a sweet-looking latter-day-
hippie type—the type that gave KC the heebie-

jeebies. KC didn't have anything against hippies. But her own parents had been sixties flower children, and Dahlia, to her, looked exactly like what her parents would have wanted *her* to be—and nothing remotely resembling the person KC would ever want to look like in a million years.

Dahlia's fine blond hair hung to her shoulders. Her big brown eyes were large and fringed with pale-blond lashes. As Cody spoke, she watched him with an expression that struck KC as exceptionally vague.

"Did KC mention her idea for a Mountain Supply promo?" Cody asked.

"No," Hindemann answered, looking at KC for clarification.

Cody looked at her too.

It was coming back now. What was the idea? Something about . . .

"In a nutshell, it's like this," Cody said, correctly reading her blank look and jumping in. He proceeded to sketch out KC's plan for Mountain Supply loaning the station some paraphernalia in exchange for plugs. "We think this Alice and Gustav Mulch bit is going to be very popular. Very humorous. The kind of thing that people will remember."

"Along with the name *Mountain Supply*," Joel added eagerly. "It's smart marketing."

KC's brains were beginning to unscramble a little. Mr. Hindemann was looking interested. The looks he was throwing KC were less dour now and he seemed a little impressed. "This was your idea?"

"That's right," Cody said, smiling at KC. "KC knows her demographics. We reach a huge number of listeners, and Mountain Supply would be reaching those listeners too."

"Not just listeners," KC corrected, now psyched and ready to plunge in. "Viewers, too. Don't forget, Ted Markham is going to be doing a video of the bit."

"Right," Joel said. "But how do we expand the life of the video? How do we get it into people's hands?"

"Dupe a bunch of cheap copies and sell them for cost out of the bookstore," Cody suggested.

"Okay. But why would people want to buy it?" Joel pressed.

"Because they're in it!" KC answered, with a burst of inspiration.

Dahlia blinked in confusion. "Huh?"

"Bumbershoot means umbrella," KC explained. "What about getting a bunch of cheap umbrellas with *Mountain Supply* written on them? ACE Wholesale Monogram, Inc., does stuff like that, and they're just a couple of blocks away. If we place the order this afternoon, we could have the umbrellas in here by tomorrow morning. We'll give them away free with every thirty-dollar purchase, or sell them for five dollars apiece. The station can announce the giveaway and also tell people that anybody who shows up at the Rain or Shine Picnic on Saturday with a Mountain Supply umbrella can be in the video."

"I get it," Joel cried. "So they buy the video because they're in it. And every time they watch it to see themselves, they see MOUNTAIN SUPPLY in every crowd scene."

"At the end of the tape, KC could step in and do a straightforward pitch for Mountain Supply," Cody finished.

KC, Cody, and Joel all did a silly three-way high-five.

"You're brilliant," Joel said, grinning at KC.

"You're right," KC joked. She felt slightly giddy from the excitement.

Even Mr. Hindemann was looking flushed and excited. He grabbed Joel's hand and began to pump it. "This is great. I'm impressed. You kids have put together a whole publicity campaign."

Joel grinned. "Now, let's talk for a moment about what we're going to need from Mountain Supply for props and costumes." He reached into his shirt pocket and pulled out a little notebook and pen. "I started a list."

Dahlia leaned over Joel's arm as he conferred with Hindemann, looking at the list and suggesting additions.

KC began to breathe easier. Hindemann seemed to have forgotten that he was just about to fire her. It looked as though her job was safe for the present, and it was all due to Cody.

She threw him a grateful look and caught him staring at her, wearing a conspiratorial smile. "You did a nice job of selling that," he said in a low tone.

"We always did make a good team," KC said softly.

He reached out and squeezed her hand. KC longed to throw her arms around him, but the others had concluded their conversation. Suddenly Joel and Dahlia were both talking at once and reminding Cody that they were due back at the station.

Cody backed up and let KC's fingers slip from his grasp. "We'll talk more later," he promised.

In his crisp way, Joel nodded good-bye and hustled Cody toward the door. Dahlia waved vaguely and wafted out behind them.

As KC watched, they crossed the street and climbed into Joel's car. Seconds later the car pulled out into the street, and KC caught a glimpse of Brooks and Angela Beth strolling down the sidewalk.

The sight of Brooks and Angela Beth seemed to sober KC and Hindemann both. KC sighed and steeled herself. There was no point in postponing the inevitable conversation about the phone company. Hindemann's good moods were usually short-lived. It wouldn't be long before his bonhomie evaporated and left him surlier than he was before. Sooner or later he was going to demand an explanation.

"Did you want to talk to me?" she asked quietly.

Hindemann stared at her for a long moment, then he shrugged. "It can wait," he said indifferently. "You might as well get back to work."

"Yes, sir," she said happily, hurrying back toward the display window. *Angeletti up one,* she thought happily. *Baldwin down one.* Her stock was high with Hindemann. And not even a consummate tale-telling, back-stabbing, rock-climbing dunderhead like Brooks could get her fired.

"KC!"

She stopped and turned. "Yes?"

"I'll be watching you," Hindemann said levelly.

She smiled. "Yes, sir." Then she climbed in the window, completely nonplussed. Hindemann could watch her all day long. Big deal. She had nothing to hide.

Besides, nothing could dampen her good mood now. Cody hadn't come by Mountain Supply just to set up a promotion. He had come because he wanted to follow up with KC, wanted to see her and talk to her.

KC moved the red lantern off the camp table and hung it over the bear's arm. Winnie was wrong, wrong, wrong, she thought happily. Cody might be into honesty, but he was still a guy. A guy whose feelings had been bruised pretty badly. He wasn't going to come right out and ask her to get back together. He was going to test the waters first. Take her temperature. Get his bearings before making the big move.

It was going to happen, though. No doubt about it. She and Cody were destined to get back together. She was sure of it.

Eight

ngela Beth watched Brooks's heavily muscled legs swing toward the surface of the Rock. The Rock was a huge cement slab formed with cracks and crevices, simulating the side of a mountain. It was located near the athletic complex, and the students used it to practice climbing techniques.

At the top was a flat ledge. At the bottom was a sawdust pit. Both Angela Beth and Brooks wore ropes and safety harnesses.

Brooks's roommate, Barney Sharfenberger, and another fraternity brother of theirs, Ed Kirkland, stood at the bottom of the rock, holding safety ropes so that if either Brooks or Angela fell, they could take up the slack and keep them from plummeting to the ground.

The rain had let up earlier, and for the first time in days, the sun was out. Still, it had taken all of Angela Beth's powers of persuasion to lure Brooks out for a practice climb. It was Tuesday afternoon, and ever since their trip to Mountain Supply the previous day, he had been remote, withdrawn, and unresponsive.

He was angry with her for pushing him to tell Hindemann about KC and the phone company. But he'd get over it. Just like he'd gotten over being angry with her for talking him into informing on KC to the phone company in the first place.

Angela Beth bit her lips to hide a little secret smile. She knew how to handle Brooks.

Pretending that she was struggling for purchase, Angela Beth began to skitter her feet along the side of the Rock. She let out a little groan of frustration. Brooks glanced over at her, but his gaze was uninterested and a tad resentful. He didn't move to help her the way he once would have.

Okay. So he wasn't going to fall right into her lap. He was going to act cold. But he couldn't keep it up for long.

She let out a little yelp of frustration. When Brooks looked in her direction again, she let her full lower lip dangle in a provocative pout and she cut her eyes toward him in a sidelong glance. "Help me?" she begged in a sweet voice. "Please?"

"If I help you, it won't do anything to improve your climbing skills," Brooks said flatly. Then he turned away and continued up the rock.

Angela Beth gritted her teeth and planted her foot in a crevice, pushing off as she climbed upward. The sweet and helpless approach didn't seem to be working. It was time to switch to the direct. "The second Bumbershoot dance is on Friday," she said softly. "Any chance I could talk you into going with me?"

Brooks shook his head. "Probably not," he answered tersely. "Dancing's not my strong suit."

Angela Beth let out a fluttery laugh. "Dancing's just hugging to music."

Brooks said nothing, but grunted as he hoisted himself up to the top of the Rock, pulling himself up on the ledge. He stood there panting, looking out over the campus. Angela Beth hoisted herself up beside him and stood. "It might be fun," she said in a sexy whisper.

He looked at her in confusion for a moment. "What might be fun?"

Angela Beth felt like stamping her foot and screaming, "The dance, you big dolt!" But she forced her mouth into a teasing smile. "Brooks," she purred. "We were talking about dancing."

A veil seemed to come down over Brooks's eyes, and he looked wary, secretive, almost as if he were afraid of her. "I'm going to the Mount Crinsley picnic grounds pretty early on Saturday morning," he said, refusing to meet her eye. "To watch the Nature Twins interview."

"Maybe I'd like to go too," Angela Beth said in a breathy tone.

Brooks shrugged. "You don't need an invitation from me. Half the school will be there. Haven't you been listening to the plugs on KRUS?"

Angela Beth put her arm around his neck and stood up on her tiptoes to breathe into his ear. "Don't be so standoffish," she teased. She could feel his heart give a heavy thump beneath his shirt, and the vein in his neck began to pulse. Angela Beth turned her face away so he wouldn't see her smile. He couldn't resist her. Not when she was this close.

She turned her face back toward his and pulled his head down to meet hers. They kissed for a long moment at the top of the Rock, and soon Brooks's arms were wound tightly around her waist.

Angela Beth drew back her head and turned it slightly away as Brooks tried to kiss her again.

"What's the matter?" he asked.

Angela Beth shook her head slightly and pouted. "I don't feel like I'm important to you anymore."

Brooks groaned. "Angela Beth, I can't keep

proving it over and over and over. Especially when it means turning on my old friends."

"But you haven't proved it at all," Angela Beth protested. "Every little thing I've asked you to do for me, you've argued with me about." She smiled. "And if your *old friends* are KC Angeletti and that crew, how can you blame me for feeling slighted? I just don't see how you can defend someone like that. Did you know she's ripping off the housing office now?"

"Angela Beth . . ." Brooks groaned.

Angela Beth studied his face, considering the wisdom of her next move. She could see the hunger in his eyes, and his arms were still wrapped around her. He might argue with what she wanted him to do, but if she played it right, he would probably do it.

She pressed her body closer to his and felt his arms tighten. "Christine Van Diem, my sorority sister, is still friendly with Marielle Danner, KC's hallmate. According to Marielle, KC has an illegal roommate in her single dorm room." She began to walk her fingers up his arm. "I don't think she should be allowed to get away with that . . . do you?"

Brooks's hungry eyes turned hostile, and he released her so abruptly, she almost fell. "Brooks!" she cried.

"Shut up!" he yelled. "Just shut up. I know what you're trying to get me to do, and you can forget it."

"Why not?" she demanded. "You told Hindemann about KC and the phone company yesterday."

"No, I didn't," he said, panting. "All I did was tell him the hiking boots in the window were overpriced. That same brand is in all the catalogs for about thirty percent less."

Angela Beth couldn't believe it. He had promised her he was going to tell Hindemann about KC's past. And he hadn't done it. He had actually *defied her*.

He gave her a nasty, sarcastic smile. "Surprised?"

"You're teasing me," she said, refusing to believe it. "You did tell Hindemann, I know you did. I heard him call KC over and say he wanted to talk to her privately."

"Probably because he heard you chewing her out for handing out climbing advice when she didn't know anything about the sport. I worked in a sporting-goods store once in high school. All the salespeople were told to give advice only if they knew what they were talking about. Otherwise they could jeopardize the store's reputation and credibility." Brooks lifted his chin defiantly. "I just hope KC didn't get into any trouble because of you. I've caused her enough trouble for both of us."

"I can't believe you!" Angela Beth screeched angrily. She felt as if the top of her head were about to come off, she was so frustrated. What was the matter with Brooks? Why couldn't he see what was right in front of his eyes? Why was his whole sense of loyalty so misplaced? "KC Angeletti is a lowlife, lying, cheating . . ." she started again.

Brooks let out a ferocious snarl and lifted his hand. "Stop it!" he roared. "I can't listen to this stuff anymore."

For a horrible moment, Angela Beth thought he was going to hit her. She screamed and ducked as his hand flew in her direction. But at the last minute his hand veered away, and . . .

Bang!

. . . smacked the backboard of the Rock.

She saw his face contort as he struggled to get a grip on his emotions. Then he squatted down, slid over the edge, and began to slide down the rope toward the bottom.

"Brooks!" she shouted. "Wait!"

But Brooks was already in the sand pit, brushing the sawdust off of his clothes. He nodded curtly to Barney and Ed and shrugged himself out of the harness.

"I can't get down by myself," Angela Beth tried, counting on his sense of chivalry.

He turned his face up. "You can stay up there and rot for all I care," he yelled.

She saw Barney and Ed both gasp in surprise and then exchange an embarrassed look.

Tears of rage, anger, and humiliation began to course down Angela Beth's cheeks. *How dare he? How dare he?* her mind screamed as she began carefully working her way down the Rock. How had their relationship deteriorated? What had happened to make him turn so stubborn and perverse? They used to share all the same feelings about honesty and integrity. What had happened to the Brooks Baldwin whose code of honor was just as solid as hers? How had that KC Angeletti managed to warp his values so completely?

By the time she reached the bottom, Angela Beth had come to a decision. She dried her tears and composed her face while she thanked Barney and Ed for their help. She even managed to plaster a smile on her face as she crossed the campus on her way back to her dorm.

She nodded her head to a blond surfer type who had cast admiring glaces her way in Spanish class. She called a greeting to a girl from her floor who was on her way into the Student Union.

But all the time she was smiling and waving, her resolve was hardening. Lots of guys temporarily lost their moral bearings. It was up to their friends to make sure they did their duty, lived up to the code.

As soon as she was inside her dorm, she quickened her steps, practically taking the stairs at a run. The sooner she acted, the sooner KC Angeletti would be discredited, and the sooner Brooks would come to his senses.

When she reached her room, she saw that her roommate was gone. That was fine. She needed to concentrate.

She pulled a sheet of paper and a pen from her desk drawer and sat down at her desk. She tapped the pen against her white teeth for a moment, then started to write to the housing office.

The words flowed right out of her. A few concise sentences informed them that KC Angeletti had, for some time, been housing an illegal roommate. And that roommate showed no signs of seeking other housing.

And she signed it . . . *Brooks Baldwin.*

Melissa shook out her bright-green rain slicker as she walked down the hall toward Danny's room. Danny had an art-survey course on Tuesday evenings, but he was usually back in his room by eight.

When she reached his door, she whipped off the matching green rain hat and shook out her short red hair, mussing it with her fingers to fluff it.

She hadn't seen Danny since the big blowup. She hoped that he had cooled down enough to talk to her. The cartoons were a hit, but that wasn't the point. The point was that she didn't have any right to ignore his feelings and wishes. She hoped he was ready to accept her apology.

The radio was playing softly on the other side of the door. When Melissa knocked, the volume was immediately lowered. "Come in," he called.

She pushed the door open and saw him sitting at his desk, his head bent over a textbook. The desk light created a halo of light around his profile. Melissa's heart thumped and she almost gasped. Sometimes she forgot how heartbreakingly handsome he was. Long, straight nose. Square chin. High cheekbones.

"I'm sorry," she said.

"I know," he said without looking up.

"Still mad?"

His lips disappeared as he considered the question. "Yeah. I think I am." He chuckled reluctantly and finally looked up. "That doesn't mean I'm not still crazy about you, though."

Melissa smiled and stepped inside. "That's a relief."

He stuck a pencil behind his ear, leaned back, and clasped his hands behind his head, stretching the muscles of his shoulders. "Let's forget it," he suggested in a brisk tone that told her he didn't want to talk about it anymore. "What's new with you? Seen Faith or Ted lately?"

Melissa sat down on the edge of the bed. "I saw Faith today, briefly. She said she couldn't stop to talk. She wanted to get back to her room in case Stephanie called or came by."

Danny dropped his hands to the wheels of his chair, and his upper body rocked slightly. "That situation is not good."

"I got that impression. Have you talked to Ted?"

"Not since Sunday night. I haven't talked to anybody since Sunday night."

"Why not?"

"I'm cultivating a reputation for being reclusive . . . and I'm too embarrassed to go out."

"Danny," Melissa sighed in frustration, "I just don't understand you. I can see why you would still be mad at me for going behind your back. But I can't understand why you'd be embarrassed about the cartoons. I mean, they're such a big hit."

Danny's head snapped in her direction. "What did you say?" he demanded.

Melissa faltered. Had she said the wrong thing again? "I just said . . ." Her nervous voice trailed off. His face looked so stern, so intense, she didn't have the nerve to keep talking.

"You said *they're a hit*. Is that what you said? I thought that's what I heard you say," he pressed in an urgent tone.

Melissa's jaw dropped. *He didn't know.* He really didn't. He wasn't mad, he was surprised. "According to Dash," she said in a level voice, " 'Wheelchairs in Outer Space' has almost knocked Alice and Gustav Mulch off the front pages. The paper has gotten tons of letters and phone calls."

"Letters and phone calls from people saying they *like* it?" Danny asked, his blue eyes flickering with disbelief, and a shy smile playing around the corners of his mouth. "They *laughed*?"

"According to Dash, they like it. And they laughed."

Danny cocked his head. "Dash is fooling you," he said curtly. "He's got to be."

"Ask him if you don't believe me," Melissa insisted.

A sudden knock at the door surprised them both.

"Come in," Danny barked.

The door opened and a tall, good-looking guy with neatly combed dark hair came in. His eyes circled the room, rested for a moment on the wheelchair, then moved to Danny's face. He gave Danny a tentative smile. "Are you Danny Markham?"

"What's left of him."

The guy looked shocked for a moment. Then he laughed appreciatively. "You're him, all right."

Melissa tried to think who this guy was. He looked really familiar.

"I'm B.W. Gonzales," the guy said with a smile, reaching out to shake Melissa's hand, then Danny's. "I'm the student-body president."

Of course. She'd seen him at freshman orientation. He was the senior who had given a short talk on university life.

"Why are you here shaking hands?" Danny asked. "You've already won the election."

B.W. grinned, then began to laugh.

"It wasn't that funny," Danny said dryly.

"Sorry. I just can't help it. You've got a sense of humor that really gets to me. Every time I think about those cartoons in the paper I get giggly all over again. I guess you're used to this, huh?"

Danny raised his eyebrows. "Not really."

"I know you're wondering what I'm doing here, so I'll cut to the chase. I've been a college student for four years, and 'Wheelchairs in Outer Space' is the most original and provocative statement on student life I've ever seen. I know the characters are in wheelchairs, but in a very humorous way, it speaks eloquently about the pain of being different. I think that's a pretty universal emotion for most college freshmen."

Danny's lips moved slightly and he stared at B.W. with an expression of interest tinged with confusion. "You think they're funny?" he asked tentatively.

Melissa put her hand to her lips to hide her smile. Danny's interest in eloquent statements and universal emotions was somewhere between zip and zilch. At heart, he was a cartoonist. All he wanted to know was . . . *are they funny?*

B.W. began to laugh again. "Funny? They're hysterical."

Danny looked torn, as if he wanted to believe B.W. was telling the truth but was afraid of finding out that he was somehow being made the butt of an elaborate joke.

"That's why the student council wanted me to ask you to introduce Gary Bartlett when he comes to the U of S to speak Friday afternoon. Just a short opening talk. You know what I mean. Something funny. To the point."

"Gary Bartlett, the cartoonist?" Danny croaked. "He's coming here?"

Gary Bartlett's strip was the hippest, funniest syndicated cartoon series in the country. It was extremely political and very popular with college students.

B.W. nodded. "That's right. Didn't you read about it in the paper? It's part of the Bumbershoot activities lineup."

Twenty different emotions crossed Danny's face, all of them happy. He looked at Melissa. He looked at B.W. His body rocked for a few moments while he struggled with his feelings.

"So will you do it?" B.W. pressed. "You'd really be helping us out, Danny. I mean, we've got all kinds of writers around the campus, but no humorists up to Bartlett's weight, besides you."

Danny schooled his face into an expression of appropriately blasé comic cool. "Sure," he said, nodding. "Why not? I guess I could make the time."

B.W. reached over and slapped his arm. "All right! I'll spread the word. Look for the fliers to be out tomorrow. *U of S humorist Danny Markham presents Gary Bartlett*." He lifted his hand and waved at Melissa.

Melissa lifted her fingers and shot him an acknowledging smile.

The door closed and Melissa waited, unsure of what to do now. Danny looked happy, but he was so volatile these days, she was afraid to say anything, afraid of tipping his precariously balanced emotions.

Danny stared off into space, his eyes focused somewhere over Melissa's head. His upper body rocked with more animation—always an indication that his mind was fully engaged. Then the hands hit the wheels and the chair spun three hundred and sixty degrees. "All right!" he shrieked.

He held out his arms and Melissa flew toward him, throwing her arms around him and laughing. "Still mad at me?"

"Yes," he chortled. "I am."

"But you're crazy about me anyway, aren't you?"

Danny ran his hand over his head and opened his eyes wide. "I'm not sure. You realize I'm on the spot now? I mean, really on the spot."

"You'll be great," Melissa insisted. She leaned forward and kissed him. "I have faith."

Nine

KC put her hands over her ears and bent her head over her open textbook. It seemed as if Winnie had been talking and fidgeting for hours—restlessly rearranging her piles of junk while keeping up a steady stream of self-deprecating "Winnie-speak."

". . . I don't know why I can't seem to get it together," she was babbling. ". . . with me, losing important papers and things is like a disease, or a curse. Maybe the psych department would give me a grant to conduct a study on myself to figure out why I'm always losing important stuff like Dining Commons passes and . . ."

KC tightened her hands over her ears. The clock said seven thirty, but it seemed a lot later. KC yawned. She'd almost forgotten how fatiguing Winnie could be. And how disturbingly perceptive.

When she'd gotten back from Mountain Supply yesterday, Winnie had taken one look at her and deduced that she had seen Cody. She'd asked a dozen questions about his visit to Mountain Supply, then warned KC all over again about getting her hopes up. KC had promised Winnie that she wasn't getting her hopes up. But she was. She couldn't help it. Deep down, in her heart of hearts, she was convinced that she and Cody belonged together. If only she could get Cody to admit that he felt the same way, get him to drop that mask of friendly indifference and deep reserve.

She couldn't believe how much she missed him. Why? Why? Why had she been so stupid? Why did she have to lose her grip and light into him like that at the auction? She gritted her teeth angrily.

It had been Brooks's fault. If it weren't for Brooks, she and Cody would still be together. If only she could get back at him somehow.

Suddenly a long scarf engulfed KC's head.

"Winnie!" KC protested, angrily extricating herself from the shimmery evening scarf that had wrapped itself around her head and neck.

"Sorry," Winnie said quickly. She was pawing through a pile of clothes on the floor like a dog pawing in sand. Garments, books, and toys were flying in all directions.

"What are you looking for?"

"The copy of my room-wanted ad," Winnie answered. "I really am going to start looking for a room of my own. I promise."

KC nodded. She'd heard that before. But she wasn't going to push Winnie to leave. Winnie might be a little trying at times, but at least she was loyal, unlike Brooks Baldwin.

What had made him change so? What had made him turn on all his old friends—especially KC?

Her mind wandered for a few moments, re-membering their old high-school crowd and all the fun they had had together. Their circle had expanded since coming to the U of S. Expanded to include Lauren and Dash and Ted and Melissa and Danny and . . .

"Winnie," she said suddenly, getting an idea.

"Yeah?"

"Don't you think it might be fun to get every-body together to do something on Saturday? Maybe go hiking on Mount Crinsley after the pic-nic and the Nature Twins interview."

"Who's *everybody*?" Winnie asked, pulling a piece of paper out of the garbage can and squint-ing at it.

"You. Me. Dash. Lauren. Faith and Ted. Most of us have to be there anyway, for the interview. Why not make a plan for afterward?"

Winnie blew out her breath in disgust, balled up the piece of paper, and dropped it back in the trash can. Clearly it was not what she was looking for. "Do I detect a hidden motive?" she asked, getting down on her hands and knees and reaching under KC's bed for a balled-up piece of notebook paper.

"What do you mean?"

Winnie flattened her body against the floor, and her head and shoulders disappeared under the bed. "I mean, getting a group together to do something is a perfect setup if you want to ask somebody to do something but don't want them to think you're singling them out for attention, if you get what I mean, and I think you do."

Winnie scootched back out from under the bed, uncrumpled the piece of paper, then twisted her mouth into a disappointed scowl.

KC stared at Winnie. How could somebody who looked so crazy sound so sane? Winnie was wearing a sheepskin vest over bicycle shorts and a huge U of S sweatshirt. On her head was a cafeteria worker's paper hat. On her feet she had on two different boots.

KC did know exactly what Winnie meant, but she wasn't going to give Winnie the satisfaction of admitting it. "I need climbing experience if I'm going to keep my job," KC insisted, tucking the tail of her red and black flannel shirt into the waistband of her jeans. "And Mount Crinsley has some easy hiking paths. None of us would need any special equipment."

Winnie rolled her eyes skeptically. "Oh, okay," she said in a voice that said, "I'm humoring you."

There was a knock on the door and Winnie hopped up and opened it. A student mail carrier stood in the doorway with an InterUniversity mail envelope in his hand. "Letter for KC Angeletti," he said.

"That's me," KC said curiously, getting up to take the letter. "Thanks."

He handed her the letter with a smile, then hurried away with his mail sack.

"I'll bet this is about the work-study application I turned in a while ago," KC said. "I don't need a job now, though." She put her nail against the flap of the envelope. But before she could slit it open, she saw Cody coming down the hall. "Hi, there!" she said happily.

Cody smiled and paused. "Hi, KC. Hi, Winnie." As usual, he was dressed in jeans, a denim shirt, and cowboy boots. Winnie smiled hello and then discreetly withdrew into the room.

"I'm glad to see you," Cody said, pulling a long envelope from his back pocket. "I was just—"

"I'm glad to see you too," KC blurted out, too overjoyed to see him to let him finish. "We were just talking about taking a group hike after the Nature Twins interview. Interested in joining us?"

"A hike?" Cody made a clicking sound in the back of his throat as he appeared to be thinking. "A hike sounds like fun, but it'll depend on how long the interview runs. I've got to be back at the station pretty early. So I'll let you know on Saturday. Okay? In the meantime . . ."

"No problem," KC said quickly, sensing his withdrawal. "Did you come by to tell me something?"

Cody scratched his chin with the corner of the long envelope. "Actually, I was just on my way out. I was in Dahlia's room. I needed to get together with her on the format for tomorrow's news breaks."

"Oh," KC answered, trying hard to keep the disappointment out of her voice.

"But I'm glad I ran into you, because I did want to talk about your Mountain Supply pitch. Joel's still got to get some approvals on this, but you might as well take a look at the preliminary copy." He took a piece of paper out of the envelope and held it out for her to look at.

KC nodded and did her best to appear to be listening as he ran his finger down the page and explained the notes that Joel had made in the margin. He was being so businesslike. Was it because he really wasn't interested in having a personal conversation with her? Or was it because

Winnie was hovering in the background with big ears, making him feel self-conscious?

The door behind Cody opened, and Marielle Danner appeared in the doorway, swaying slightly. She was drunk. Or stoned. "Excuse me," she slurred, coming out into the narrow hallway on her way to the bathroom. But as she tried to pass behind Cody, she stumbled and fell against him.

The weight of her body forced him forward. Somehow, in his effort to keep his balance and keep KC from falling too, his arms wound up around her and she found herself pressed up against his chest.

"Sorry," Marielle muttered, haughtily tossing her hair off of her shoulders and moving down the hall.

KC's heart skipped a beat, and she felt a flutter at the base of her spine when she looked up and saw Cody's handsome face bending over hers. His arms tightened for a moment and KC felt the same thrill of electricity she had always felt in his embrace. Cody felt it too, she realized joyously. The deep-red flush of embarrassed confusion on his face told her that he did. If cool, calm, and collected Cody was losing his composure, it meant his emotions were threatening to overwhelm him.

She smiled mistily. "Cody," she whispered.

Abruptly he released her. "I've got to, uh . . . got to go," he stuttered in confusion. He fumbled for a moment with the paper and the envelope. "Here," he said, thrusting them into her hand. "Look it over and call Joel if you have any questions."

"Cody!" she cried.

But he was already gliding down the hall, his long legs carrying him down the wide oak staircase.

KC smiled. No point in getting upset. It was going to take him a little time to get used to the idea that he still had feelings for her. But he would get used to it. And maybe he would join them for the hike. Then maybe the two of them would hike off on their own, and . . .

Her mind began spinning a happy fantasy in which she and Cody were wrapped in each other's arms with the romantic backdrop of Mount Crinsley behind them.

"What's in the University letter?" Winnie asked, appearing at her shoulder.

"Oh." KC smiled. "I forgot about the letter." She handed Cody's envelope to Winnie to hold, and slit the InterUniversity envelope with her nail. "Probably just a letter telling me there still aren't any campus jobs but they'll keep me in their files," she murmured, removing two folded pieces of paper. But as her eyes began to scan the page, they grew wider. "That weasel!" she bellowed.

Winnie stepped back in shocked surprise. "What's wrong?"

KC's hands were shaking with rage. "It's from the housing office," she told Winnie through gritted teeth. "It has, quote, come to their attention that I have an illegal roommate. I have one week to *rectify the situation* before they *take action.*"

Winnie's eyes grew large and her fingers danced nervously on the top of her spiky hairdo. "I'm sorry," she said quickly. "I'm really, really sorry."

"It's not your fault," KC fumed. She thrust one of the pieces of paper under Winnie's nose. "Here's the copy of the letter that informed on us. Look at the signature."

Winnie's worried eyes focused on the letter. Then she gasped and snatched it from KC's hand, bringing it up so close to her face that her nose was almost pressed against it. "I don't believe it. *Brooks Baldwin?*"

"Why is he doing this?" KC shouted at the top of her voice. She backed into her room and slammed the door shut.

She was so angry, so furious, and so enraged that she savagely kicked the metal garbage can, denting the side and sending it skidding across the floor. "He's ruining my life. He broke up my relationship with Cody. He tried to get me fired. Now he's trying to get me thrown off campus!"

"What are you going to do?" Winnie asked in a frightened whisper.

KC took a deep breath and struggled to get her temper back under control. "I don't know," she said in a shaking voice. "But it's time to start fighting back. Time to let the world know what kind of sick, evil person Brooks really is."

Ten

"**D**ismissed!"

The professor closed his notebook with a brisk snap and stepped down from the podium at the front of the large lecture auditorium.

The Thursday-afternoon western civilization section was a huge class with over a hundred students. Now that class was over, they laughed and talked among themselves as they collected their books, located their umbrellas, and began filing out. Within seconds the cavernous room was echoing with noise. In spite of the racket, Winnie could see Faith sleeping soundly at the end of their row, her cheek resting in her hand.

Winnie elbowed Lauren, who elbowed KC, who elbowed Faith. Faith's eyes flew open, blinked, then focused on the three girls who were leaning forward in the aisle and giggling.

"If you're through napping," Winnie joked, "you might get up so we can leave."

Faith gave them an embarrassed grin and reached under her seat for her book bag. "Sorry. It was a late night last night."

"Stephanie?" Lauren asked.

Faith nodded and stood. "She was in my room all night."

Winnie followed the other three girls up the aisle to the exit door. As they walked down the long white corridor covered with Junior Year Abroad posters, Winnie noticed that everyone seemed to be yawning.

"I've got to hit the snack bar and get some coffee," Faith mumbled as they all stepped outside into the gray weather. "Anybody else headed in that direction?"

"I am," Lauren said.

"I'll walk with you guys as far as the library," KC offered. "Winnie? You coming?"

Winnie shook her head and pulled at the neck of her gray pullover sweater. It was enormous and practically hung to the knees of the baggy black shorts she wore over her tights. "I've got some stuff to do," she answered vaguely. She hoped they wouldn't ask her what. She didn't feel like explaining that she was going to the Hotline.

She didn't need to worry. Nobody questioned her. Winnie could tell they were all too preoccupied with their own problems to be curious about hers right now.

Faith was all involved with Stephanie. KC was busy thinking about Cody and raging about Brooks. And Lauren's whole focus was on the Nature Twins script she and Dash were writing.

As they waved and drifted off, Winnie realized going to the Hotline was the right move. She had to quit depending so much on her friends for support. She needed to develop more independence and stop making *her* problems *their* problems.

Step one was finding a room of her own. That would get KC off the hook. The bulletin board at the Hotline was a great place to advertise. And maybe answering a few phones while she was there would help her get her own head straightened out.

Winnie's eyes studied the toes of her waterproof combat boots as she splashed her way across campus and down the street toward the Hotline headquarters. She couldn't seem to shake the vague depression that made her feet feel so heavy and her arms and legs seem so tired.

Maybe it was the weather. Nonstop rain and clouds were enough to depress anyone.

No. It was her life. Why shouldn't she be depressed? She was still only a freshman in college, and look at everything she had been through. She'd gotten married, gotten pregnant, had a miscarriage, lost her husband to another woman, wound up with no place to live except KC's room. And now even that was being taken away from her.

By the time Winnie made her way to downtown Springfield and reached the Crisis Hotline Center, a sob had risen in her throat and a few tears were trickling down her cheek.

Cut it out, she ordered herself sternly. *Hotline counselors are not allowed to bawl while on duty.* She swallowed the lump, wiped away the tears, and opened the glass door.

Six people sat at a long counter, manning the phones. But only two of the six were engaged in telephone conversations. The other four were leaning back in their seats, shooting rubber bands across the room and chatting quietly.

Obviously the Hotline was not being besieged with callers. The two who were engaged in counseling held the receivers close to their faces and spoke in low, soothing tones.

Tina, a senior psychology major who was speaking on one of the phones, smiled and waved hello to Winnie. Then she pointed to the empty chair beside her, telling her to man that phone when she got ready. Winnie nodded. "I'll be there in a minute," she mouthed.

First she wanted to post her ad and study the

bulletin board. Winnie pulled the neatly lettered index card from her pocket and her eyes searched the board for a spare thumbtack. There were a lot of roommate wanted signs.

"Wanted. Nonsmoking female. Own bedroom. Separate bath."

That sounded good. But what if she suddenly decided to take up smoking? Sure, it wasn't good for you. But who wanted to live with some control freak who wouldn't even let her smoke if she wanted to? Forget it. No way.

"Wanted. Female student to share three-bedroom house with yard. Must be neat."

Nope. That ruled her out.

"Must provide own furniture."

Nope.

"No pets."

Winnie didn't have any. But she didn't want to live with somebody who didn't like animals.

Who *were* all these people? Where did all these controlling, authoritarian, animal-hating, clean freaks come from? She didn't want to live with any of these people. Not in a million years. And she didn't want them calling her, either.

Winnie crumpled the index card in her fist, then jumped when somebody tapped her on the shoulder. She whirled around, and to her utter amazement found herself face to face with Stephanie.

Stephanie's face was pale and her eyes were red

rimmed. She looked a lot younger than sixteen today. Maybe it was because she was wearing the plaid skirt and white blouse that were the uniform at St. Mary's, the all-girl high school she attended.

Winnie looked at the clock. It wasn't anywhere near three o'clock yet.

"I cut school this afternoon," Stephanie volunteered.

"Well . . ." Winnie said.

"I just couldn't stand it today," Stephanie said quietly. "I know you said not to ask for you if I called here, but I couldn't remember the number anyway. So I decided to come by. And then I saw you and . . ." Her voice was gruff with tears. "I . . . uh . . . just needed to talk to somebody," she added.

It had been so long since anyone had reached out to Winnie for help, she didn't know quite how to respond. All the old nurturing and caring responses were a little rusty. But Winnie figured she could probably fake it. "Sure," she said encouragingly. "Let's sit down and talk. Come on over here."

Stephanie followed her to a secluded corner of the room. They sat down and stared at each other awkwardly. Neither one of them said a word, and the silence seemed to go on and on until Winnie decided she couldn't stand it anymore. "Well?"

"Well what?"

"What's the problem?" Winnie asked gently.

"That's what I want you to tell me," Stephanie responded in a frustrated voice. "I need somebody to tell me why I feel so completely alone. And why I hate every guy I see. And why my father thinks the right thing for me to do is go to the police station on Saturday and tell them to forget the whole thing. What's wrong with me? Why is my life so awful? I mean, what did I do to deserve this?" she finished, weeping quietly.

"Hoo, boy. Oh boy oh boy oh boy," Winnie breathed, stringing the words together. She reached into her pocket and produced a fresh package of tissues. "Here. You need them more than I do."

Stephanie's fingers clutched the package and her shoulders shook as she began to sob. Winnie put her arm around her. "I don't have all those answers, Stephanie," she said quietly. "Nobody who works at a telephone hotline does. We've got platitudes, we've got pep talks, we've got the number to call if you overdose on drugs. Stuff like that. But you're wasting your time here, okay? And so am I. So let's go somewhere and talk person to person. Not counselor to caller."

Stephanie nodded her agreement, and Winnie waited a few minutes while Stephanie regained a little control over her emotions. "Okay," she said, gulping. "I'm ready."

Winnie waved and mouthed the word "good-bye" to Tina, who was still on the phone. Then she took Stephanie's hand, pulling her along behind her as they left the Crisis Hotline Center.

"How about going to the Zero Bagel?" Stephanie suggested as they walked down the street toward the main shopping drag.

Winnie shook her head. "No, thanks. My soon-to-be ex-husband hangs out there, and I don't think I'm up to the strain of seeing him and his new girlfriend looking happy together."

"That sounds awful," Stephanie said.

Winnie smiled crookedly. "It is." She jerked her head toward a coffee shop that had absolutely nothing trendy, stylish, or attractive about it. "How about that place?" Winnie asked. "I never see anybody from campus going in. Mostly it looks like retired people hang out there. We won't see anybody we know, so if we start crying or something, we're okay."

Stephanie nodded and followed Winnie through the heavily stenciled glass door into the coffee shop. The air inside was heavy with the smell of coffee, cigarette smoke, hamburgers, and wet newspapers. It smelled exactly like what a coffee shop was supposed to smell like, and Winnie felt vaguely comforted by the predictability of the place.

A waitress wearing a blue polyester uniform stood behind the counter, leaning on her elbows and reading the sports page while puffing on a cigarette. She looked up curiously as Winnie and Stephanie passed by the long counter on their way to a booth in the back. Winnie smiled and held up two fingers. "Two coffees, please."

The waitress nodded, swiveled around, and reached languidly for the coffeepot. With her other hand she snatched two mugs from under the counter, then followed the girls to the booth, her mules slapping against her heels.

Winnie and Stephanie settled themselves in the orange plastic booth and wriggled out of their rain gear as the waitress poured their coffee and withdrew, returning to her newspaper and cigarette.

"It's not the Ritz," Winnie commented. "But the coffee smells good, and at least it's not infested with soon-to-be ex-husbands."

"Do you still love him?" Stephanie asked. "I mean, you must have loved him once. Do you still love him now?"

It was a fair and logical question. So why did it hurt so much? Winnie felt her whole body deflate and her face contort. She didn't know how she felt about Josh anymore. All she knew was that it hurt to think about him—which was maybe why she spent so little time thinking at all these days. No matter what she let her mind concentrate on, it always seemed to bring her back to Josh.

"I'm sorry," Stephanie said quickly. She reached across the table and took Winnie's hand.

"I'm really sorry. I didn't mean to make you un-happy. I shouldn't have asked you that . . . or said anything or . . . or . . . I probably should have known better, but I didn't . . . because . . . I'm just a kid," she whispered finally.

"So am I," Winnie croaked, pulling a napkin out of the napkin holder to use as a tissue. "And believe me, I say all the wrong things. Do all the wrong things. And stay awake nights worrying about all the same things you do. *What's wrong with me? Why is my life so awful? What did I do to deserve this?*"

Winnie wiped her nose. "I feel like a victim, and I don't know how to change the way I'm feeling, don't know how to get my self-esteem back." She let out a watery chuckle. "Not that I ever had any to begin with."

Stephanie laughed and wiped her nose too. "Me neither. I was real conceited. But that's not the same thing. I think I acted conceited because deep down I really didn't feel very important or special and I didn't want people to know."

Winnie raised her eyebrows. "That's very as-tute," she commented. "Very self-aware. And self-awareness is usually the first step toward solving a problem."

"Maybe," Stephanie answered, tracing the spi-dery lines of the Formica tabletop with a finger-nail. "I just wish I knew what to do about my dad and the appointment he set up for me on

Saturday with the police. Our family lawyer is supposed to go with us." Her large blue eyes appealed to Winnie. "They all want me to drop the charges. What would you do if you were me?"

Winnie sniffed and leaned her head against the back of the booth, staring at the white acoustical tiles on the ceiling.

What would she do?

"I know what my parents are like," Stephanie continued. "They'll start out fighting with me, pressuring me to back down. Then they'll start fighting with each other if I don't do what they want. Then I'll start feeling so horrible about them fighting that it'll seem easier on everybody just to do what they want, and . . ." Stephanie put her hands to the sides of her head and drummed her feet against the legs of the table. "Ohhh," she groaned in frustration. "I just don't know what to do. I don't know."

Winnie sat up straight and began rearranging the condiments. "Okay. Here's an idea. Going to the police station on Saturday is part of *their* timetable, not yours. You don't have to make any big decisions yet if you're not ready. So instead of going to the police station, why don't you and I go to Mount Crinsley? We'll meet Faith and Ted and KC. Do a little hiking and deep breathing. Clear our heads a little."

Stephanie's fingers fidgeted with the saltshaker. "I'll think about it. I'll talk to Faith and . . ."

Stephanie trailed off and was still for a moment.

"And?" Winnie prompted.

"Talking to Faith . . ." Stephanie let out a little breath of frustration. "She's great. Totally great. But . . ." Her eyes met Winnie's. "I know she doesn't understand. Not really. And it doesn't help me that much to talk to her anymore. Sometimes talking to her makes me feel *worse.*"

"I hope *I* haven't made you feel worse," Winnie said quickly, guilt constricting her heart. Some Hotline counselor she was. Stephanie had come to her for help, and wound up listening to Winnie's problems.

"No," Stephanie said in a surprised voice. "I feel better. You're the first person I've talked to in days that's made me feel like I'm not alone."

Winnie smiled. "I'm glad. So I'll see you Saturday?"

Stephanie nodded. "Yeah. Sure. I don't really need to talk to Faith about that before I decide. I'll see you Saturday." She took a sip of her coffee and her eyes smiled over the rim of her cup.

Winnie picked up her coffee cup and held it out to Stephanie as if she were making a toast. "Well, here's to us," she said, smiling. "We made a decision *by ourselves.*"

Stephanie grinned and tapped her coffee cup against Winnie's. "That's right," she agreed softly. "Here's to us."

Eleven

Danny adjusted the knot of his tie and nervously consulted the notes on his index cards. His hands were shaking slightly and his heart was racing. He couldn't believe it was Friday already.

All around him, people scurried through the backstage area, urgently whispering instructions to one another as they made last-minute adjustments to the perplexing network of ropes and pulleys that operated the curtains and the auditorium lights. He could hear the rustle and roar of the audience out front as they found their seats and talked and laughed among themselves.

He hadn't met Gary Bartlett yet. But he'd

been told the famous cartoonist was in the guest dressing room, going over his speech. He had sent a message via the stage manager that he was looking forward to meeting Danny after the program.

Danny stuffed the index cards into the inside pocket of the oversize sports coat he wore with a white button-down shirt and gray pants. He wiped his mouth with the back of his hand. He was almost sick with nervousness. In about two minutes, he was going to have to wheel himself out on that stage and face an audience of around five hundred people who had come to hear Gary Bartlett speak.

Gary Bartlett and Danny Markham.

It was amazing. Absolutely, unbelievably, amazing, the response "Wheelchairs in Outer Space" had gotten. People he'd never met stopped him on the campus to tell him how much they liked it. Girls he had never even spoken to smiled and waved at him when he wheeled past.

All that was great, he reflected, biting his knuckle. But it sure doubled the pressure on him to be funny in his introduction. God! He was terrified. He'd done a lot of public speaking in high school, had gotten laughs when he'd gone for them. But he'd done it standing up. He'd never faced an audience sitting in a wheelchair.

Suddenly there was a rustle and a lot of shushing among the people backstage. The houselights were going down, and the audience out front was suddenly quiet.

The stage manager, in his black jeans and black T-shirt, hurried over and clipped a mike to Danny's lapel. "Show time," he whispered to Danny. "Need a push?"

"No, thanks, I've already had one," he answered, mentally cursing Melissa for getting him into this.

He put his hands on the wheels. The usually rock-solid muscles of his upper arms felt like jelly. But somehow he managed to keep pushing until he left the protective cover of the curtain and wheeled out onto the stage.

The quiet audience suddenly became even quieter. Danny had never felt quite so self-conscious in his whole life. He wondered if his face looked as red as it felt.

He positioned the chair in the center of the stage and looked out over the sea of curious faces. He could feel hundreds of eyes peering at him through the dark. His mouth felt dry, as if it had been stuffed with cotton.

He could sense the audience beginning to grow uneasy. But still, he said nothing.

The silence deepened.

Danny's eyes swept across the front row, spotting several familiar faces. Liza Ruff and her boyfriend, Waldo. Dash and Lauren. Ted and Faith.

Even their faces were beginning to register un-ease as the silence went on. He forced himself to wait so that he stretched the sense of unease to the very limit of the audience's endurance. Finally he decided the time was right.

"So," he said in a silly foreign accent, cutting his eyes cunningly at the audience. "I guess you're wondering why I called you all here." It was a quote from one of the panels of "Wheelchairs In Outer Space."

The audience roared with laughter and burst into applause. The line wasn't that funny, but it released the tension and put the audience firmly on his side.

He felt himself relaxing. When he saw Melissa's face in the front row, smiling proudly, he knew it was going to be a piece of cake. He leaned back in the chair, laced his fingers across his lap, and eased into the short comic monologue he had prepared to introduce Gary Bartlett.

Melissa applauded enthusiastically along with the rest of the audience as Gary Bartlett bowed his thanks and left the stage.

She'd heard people laughing during Bartlett's talk, but she hadn't been listening. She'd been too busy savoring Danny's success, mentally replaying every line of the funny introduction he had given, and mentally listening to the laughter and ap-plause it had elicited.

"Come on," Faith whispered, appearing in the aisle behind her. "Let's hurry backstage so we can meet Bartlett and say hello to Danny. I'll show you the quick way to get there. Head toward the stage."

Melissa nodded and jumped to her feet. People were starting to stream out of the aisles now, and the two girls had to shove and jostle to work their way against the tide.

Faith led her down to the edge of the stage, then through a doorway draped with a heavy, dull purple curtain. She pulled the curtain aside and motioned to Melissa to go through.

A few more steps, and suddenly they were backstage.

Apparently they weren't the only ones who had decided to pay a backstage visit. The place was packed. Melissa stood on her toes, looking over the heads of the crowd, trying to get a glimpse of Danny. She didn't see him anywhere. Maybe he hadn't waited.

"Come on," Faith said. "Let's see if we can meet Bartlett."

"Where is he?"

Faith nodded her head in the direction of a knot of people gathered in a circle. The circle erupted into laughter. "That must be him. Come on."

"Excuse me. Excuse me. Excuse me, please." Melissa finally managed to work her way toward the knot of Bartlett admirers, but when she and Faith broke through, her jaw dropped and her eyes bulged. It wasn't Bartlett who was enjoying the admiration and adulation of the crowd—it was Danny.

He looked up and caught her eye. He smiled and his lips began forming the words "I'll meet you . . ." But before he could finish, a tall willowy brunette with hair down to her waist leaned over to speak to him. Her curtain of hair obscured Melissa's view of his face. The crowd of people moved in closer, surrounding him completely.

"Gosh." Faith grinned. "Looks like Danny's got more fans than Bartlett. You must be thrilled."

Melissa smiled. She was. She really was. And she couldn't wait to tell him.

Angela Beth sat on the edge of Brooks's desk chair in the dark. Lucky thing he rarely locked his door. Otherwise she would have had to wait for him in the hall. The way he was being these days, she wasn't sure he would even let her in.

She had been waiting for him a long time. He hadn't been at the Bartlett program, and she hadn't seen him in the Dining Commons. So she had decided to come looking for him here, at his dorm.

Rapids Hall was quiet tonight. No radios. No stereos. None of the typical jock noises that usually filled the hallways. None of the good-natured teasing. Most of the guys were probably at the dance, Angela Beth reflected.

Tick, tick, tick, went the clock on the bureau, sounding unnaturally loud in the neat, orderly room that Brooks shared with Barney Sharfenberger.

Angela reached back and released her thick dark hair from its ponytail, letting it fall down around the shoulders of the tight green sweater that Brooks liked. She shook out her hair, fluffing it around her face, and smoothed her leggings down over her shapely legs.

Too bad she and Brooks weren't going to the dance. She looked good, and her outfit accentuated all her curves. It would have been nice to be seen on Brooks's arm and be admired. They made a great-looking couple.

But there was no sense in trying to get Brooks to the dance. She wouldn't even try. The important thing to accomplish tonight was reestablishing her relationship with him.

The door opened and Angela Beth held her breath. The light from the hallway illuminated the room briefly, but he didn't see her. He closed the door, but didn't turn on the light.

She watched his tall, broad-shouldered body bend slightly as he placed his books neatly on the desk.

He was tired. Exhausted. She could tell that

from the slump of his shoulders and the curve of his back.

She shook her head and had to fight the little flicker of contempt she felt. He was weak. That was his problem. Weak from the emotional strain of the last few days. He thought his problem was Angela Beth. Poor thing. Didn't he see that she was the only one who really wanted to help him? That she was the only one who could make him a man?

It was KC Angeletti that was the problem.

Brooks sat down on the bed with an exhausted sigh, kicked off his rubber shoes, and flopped down, sighing with fatigue.

Angela Beth stood and moved slowly toward him. "Brooks," she whispered.

"What the . . ."

Brooks started to sit up, but Angela Beth pushed him down, gently pressing against his chest. "Stay there," she ordered softly.

"Angela Beth," he groaned in a tired voice. "Go away. Please."

Angela Beth leaned over until her face was only inches away from his. Even though the room was dark, she could see his eyes and she knew he could see hers. She lowered her lashes and brushed her lips against his. "I don't like fighting with you," she purred. "I want you back."

"I can't deal with you anymore," he said wearily. "I can't deal with the pressure you put on me.

Can't deal with having all my friends despise me."

He turned his head away, but Angela Beth flattened her body down on top of his. "Won't you give me another chance?"

"It won't do any good," he said dully. "I don't like you anymore, Angela Beth. And you know what? I never did."

"I *love* you," she said quickly.

Brooks sighed but said nothing.

"Don't you care?" she asked in a throbbing tone, forcing her voice into a passionate vibrato.

Brooks shifted uncomfortably. "I don't care about much of anything right now," he answered.

"I love you," she repeated. "And I can make you care." She planted a kiss squarely on his lips.

This time, she felt him kiss her back. His arms lifted and wrapped around her waist. "We'll spend some time together this weekend," she whispered. "We'll go to the picnic together. Then we can do some climbing on Mount Crinsley. Just us. Alone. Okay?"

Brooks sighed and let his head drop back against the pillow. "Sure," he agreed wearily. "Why not?"

Angela Beth laid her head against his chest and listened to his heartbeat. He was lucky to have her. And someday, when their enemies were defeated and the two of them had nothing to fear from anyone anymore, he would realize that.

* * *

It had been a long time since Ted felt this elated. Seeing Danny knock the audience off their feet had given him as big a kick as any success of his own would have.

Faith smiled up at him as they crossed the campus on their way back from Luigi's, an off-campus Italian restaurant. He had planned to take Danny and Melissa out to dinner with them to celebrate. But Danny had been too busy with his admirers, and then Gary Bartlett had invited him to have a cup of coffee in his backstage dressing room. Melissa had said she had some things to do, and so it just hadn't worked out for them to hook up.

"That was a great dinner," Faith said. "Hope you're not too disappointed that Danny and Melissa weren't with us."

"Nah. The four of us can have dinner anytime. How often will Danny get a chance to talk one-on-one with somebody like Gary Bartlett?"

"So what do you say? Are you up for the second Bumbershoot dance?"

Ted pulled her to a stop, twirled her around, and then twirled himself around under her arm until their arms were intertwined and twisted together like a telephone cord. "Ready and willing. Let's go now and be unfashionably on time," he suggested, trying to make his voice sound light and eager.

He didn't really want to go to the dance this early, but he was afraid if they went by her dorm or his, they would run into Stephanie.

Tonight's dinner was the first time in a long time that he and Faith had been alone together, just the two of them. Talking and laughing the way they used to. Neither one of them had even mentioned Stephanie. It had made Ted realize what a dampening influence her constant presence was having on their romance.

"Let's go by my dorm first and—"

"Oops," Ted interrupted, spinning jerkily around and pretending to come untwisted. Once free, he began to laugh and pulled Faith close, covering her face with playful kisses, hoping to make her forget whatever it was she wanted to do in her room. Faith giggled happily and responded with kisses of her own. "Come on," Ted urged. "Let's go to the dance. I'm up for it, and if I don't get there before the pasta hits bottom, I'm liable to fall asleep."

"Okay," Faith agreed. "Let's go."

They joined hands and began hurrying past the dorm. The large dorm parking lot was just to the left, and the two of them were momentarily blinded by the high beams of a car as it pulled in.

Faith blinked and then started when the driver cut the lights and the silhouette of the car became visible.

Uh-oh, Ted thought, his good spirits sinking.

"Ted. That's Stephanie," Faith cried, starting off toward the parking lot.

Ted tightened his grasp on Faith's fingers and pulled her back. "Hold it a second," he said softly.

Faith turned her face up toward his. "It's *Stephanie*," she repeated.

He held up his free hand. "Let me just say something here. It won't kill Stephanie to spend one evening by herself."

"Ted!"

"Let her be alone this one time," Ted urged. "We need some time together. You know we do. And I'm not sure we're helping her."

"How can you say that?"

"Because I'm pretty sure it's true. We're not trained therapists or counselors or any of that stuff. Stephanie doesn't seem to be getting any happier or healthier. And neither are we."

Faith blew out her breath and ran her fingers through her loose hair. "Maybe you're right," she agreed reluctantly. "Maybe we do need an evening to ourselves. Let me just tell her that we need the night off."

Stephanie still hadn't spotted them, and she was climbing out of her car now. Ted felt Faith's body tense as she prepared to call out a greeting.

"Don't," he begged. "If you talk to her, we're sunk. You know we are. We'll be here all night."

Faith's eyes flickered back and forth between his face and the forlorn figure that was now trudging across the parking lot toward Faith's dormitory building.

Ted clamped his teeth together and tried hard not to get angry. Every muscle in Faith's body was on edge. She was like a mother lion, poised to go chasing after a cub who had strayed too far.

Helping people who were troubled or in trouble was so ingrained in her that it was harder for her to detach than it was for her to get involved.

Suddenly he felt like a heel. A card-carrying bad guy. The selfish boyfriend who resented seeing his girlfriend pay attention to someone else.

Forget it, he thought. Spending the evening with Faith wasn't worth having to feel this way about himself. He let go of her hand and raised both of his in a gesture of surrender. "Go on. You're right. She needs you. Go do what you think you need to do, and I'll see you later."

Faith's face was a mixture of relief and worry. "Aren't you coming?" she asked.

"I'm going to the dance," he said. "I can't help Stephanie right now. If you want to try, that's fine. But I just can't put my whole life on hold for her."

"Please don't be angry," Faith begged. "Try to understand what she's been through, and—"

"I do understand," he interrupted before she could finish her speech about how victims needed unqualified support. He couldn't listen to it again. He just couldn't. It wasn't that he didn't care, and it wasn't that he was insensitive. But there was nothing he could do about it, and he didn't understand how it helped Stephanie for him to be miserable. If there was something concrete he could do, he would be happy to do it. "You can find me at the dance if you really need me," he said softly, trying to voice his feelings without sounding harsh. "Otherwise . . ." He trailed off and shrugged his shoulders.

Faith nodded. "I'll see you tomorrow at Mount Crinsley." It was half a promise. Half a question.

He kissed her lightly on the cheek. "Sure. We'll watch the Nature Twins interview together."

Her face looked relieved, and she smiled. "I'll talk to you in the morning, then," she said, her body tense to be off.

"Right."

"Stephanie!" Faith called out, trotting into the parking lot. "Stephanie, wait up! It's me. Faith."

Ted turned away and began walking in the direction of the gym. He tried to remember if he had ever, in his whole life, been to a dance without a date before.

He hadn't.

Furthermore, he wasn't looking forward to the experience. He shoved his hands down into the pockets of his windbreaker.

Maybe it was time to rethink this whole relationship.

Twelve

....

Melissa paused in the lobby of Danny's dorm and checked her reflection in a wall mirror. After the Gary Bartlett program, she had gone back to her dorm to change into something a little more festive than the tracksuit she had worn earlier.

Tonight was a special night for Danny. And for her. She wanted her clothes and her hair and her makeup to be special.

Their relationship had almost come apart under the strain of the last few days. But now, after Danny's success, Melissa hoped that the bond between them would be stronger than ever. Surely he could forgive her now for interfering, for violating his boundaries. And maybe he wouldn't need such closely guarded boundaries anymore. The boost to his self-esteem was bound to mitigate some of the anger and fear that had created such an impenetrable wall around him.

Melissa pulled her lipstick from the pocket of her long, floral-printed challis skirt and dabbed a little more color on her lips. Her brown, green, and gold-flecked sweater brought out the gold highlights of her hair and the russet color in her cheeks. Danny liked her in this sweater, but she hadn't worn it in a long time. Fortunately the rainy season had made the evenings cool enough for sweaters again.

She ran her fingers through her red hair, tweaking the ends into curls and fluffing them out around her face. Satisfied that she looked her best, she hurried through the lobby with her heart beginning to thump a little.

It had been a long time since they'd had a romantic evening together. Too long.

"Looking for Danny?" she heard a familiar voice call out from the other side of the lobby. Melissa turned and saw Jason, Danny's RA. "Because if you are, he's not in his room," he added. "He's over at the Bumbershoot dance."

"The Bumbershoot dance?" Melissa repeated in disbelief.

"Yeah. I was just over there, and man, it's packed," Jason added.

"Are you sure?" Melissa asked. "I mean, are you sure Danny was there? It wasn't somebody else?" It was a stupid question. But she just couldn't help feeling that Jason was wrong. Danny at a dance? That was nuts. He had made his feelings about attending a dance crystal clear.

Jason grinned. "I know Danny when I see him—even though I'm not used to seeing him in a tie." He laughed.

Melissa smiled, her mind trying to reconstruct their brief communication backstage. She visualized Danny's face and tried to mentally read his lips. What had he been trying to tell her before he had disappeared from view? She had assumed he was telling her to meet him here. But maybe he had some reason for meeting her at the dance.

Still trying to fathom Danny's strange change of heart, she thanked Jason for the information and hurried out into the night. There were tons of people on the dorm green, all of them dressed to party. She followed a crowd that was streaming in the direction of the gym. The music from the dance floated out into the night and she heard it long before she saw the lights of the athletic complex.

"Hey, Melissa!" someone shouted as she passed the snack bar. Melissa turned and saw Lauren jogging to catch up with her. She was wearing red jeans with a blue sweater, and she had a paper take-out bag under her arm.

"Where's Dash?" Melissa asked.

"Dead, maybe," Lauren joked. "I just left him in the writing lab. We're working there because they have those compendiums of old jokes. We've been up for two nights now, working on our Nature Twins routine. Seeing Gary Bartlett was the only break we've taken. I just came out to get some air and pick up a fresh supply of junk food."

"How is the Nature Twins sketch going?"

"We thought it was going very nicely, until Danny totally eclipsed us in the humor department," Lauren said in mock exasperation. She took off her glasses and pinched the bridge of her nose. Melissa noticed dark circles under Lauren's large violet eyes.

"You guys have really worked hard on this routine, haven't you?"

Lauren nodded and put her glasses back on. "I'll be glad when it's finally over and we can quit rewriting and rewriting and rewriting. Humor is really not our best sport." She shot a glance at Melissa. "Do you think Danny might be willing to take a look at it? Punch it up if it needs it?"

"Come on into the athletic complex with me and you can ask him. His RA said he was at the dance."

"Danny's at the dance?" Lauren repeated in an incredulous voice. "What's he doing there?"

Melissa shrugged. "I don't know. Maybe Gary Bartlett wanted to see a real live college dance or something. Whatever he's doing, he's probably ready to leave. Come on. Let's go rescue him."

Melissa and Lauren jogged up the front steps of the athletic complex and pushed open the door. The music in the hallway was loud, and when they entered the gym, the volume was so high it practically knocked them over. Jason had been right. The place was packed.

"Maybe he's by the refreshment table," Melissa shouted. "Let's go."

But she stopped when she felt Lauren's hand close over her sleeve and tug. "Wait."

Melissa turned and saw Lauren smiling curiously and pointing toward the dance floor. "There he is."

Melissa's eyes followed Lauren's finger and then practically bulged. For somebody who had been adamant about hating dances, Danny was doing a great impression of someone having the time of his life.

His tie was loosened and the sports coat was gone. Danny's muscular shoulders moved back and forth to the pounding music, and his upper body swayed and rocked gracefully. Every once in a while, he would punctuate a drumroll by spinning the wheelchair in a circle—a move that elicited smiles and applause from the radius of dancers surrounding him.

Melissa recognized his dance partner, a petite blonde they had seen on campus a few times.

Danny had jokingly admired her a couple of times. He was smiling at her now and she was smiling at him, moving her body closer and closer to the chair.

Just as she was about to sit on Danny's lap, the tall willowy brunette from backstage tapped her on the shoulder and cut in. The blonde danced away, and the willowy brunette took her place, moving her head so that her long curtain of hair swung back and forth. She took Danny's hand, and the two of them executed an inventive jitter-bug.

"Wow!" Lauren shouted into her ear. "When Danny comes out of his shell, he really comes out."

Melissa forced herself to smile. She should feel thrilled to death to see Danny so obviously at ease and having a great time. Why wasn't she?

Danny's wheelchair turned and his blue eyes caught hers. There was about a four-second delay between eye contact and his acknowledging smile.

As far as Melissa was concerned, that was four seconds too long.

The music stopped suddenly, and the dancers applauded the music. Danny clapped his hands, said something to his dance partner, and began wheeling himself toward Melissa. "Hi!" he said, smiling. "Hey, Lauren."

Melissa gave him a tight smile in return. "Hi. Where's Gary Bartlett?"

Danny looked confused. "Gone back to his hotel, I guess. Why?"

"I thought maybe you came to the dance because he wanted to see some college life."

Danny shook he head. "Bartlett and I talked for about half an hour after the program. He said some really encouraging things. Gave me a few names to contact when I'm ready to go professional. Then he split. He said he flies back to New York early tomorrow morning. I came to the dance because Tina and Sherry begged me to come, and I hated to disappoint them."

The blonde and the brunette materialized behind Danny with glasses of punch.

"Tina. Sherry. I want you to meet a couple of my friends, Lauren Turnbell-Smythe and Melissa McDormand."

Friends!

Melissa couldn't believe it. Had Danny forgotten she was his *girl*friend?

Tina, the tall blonde, gave her a perfunctory smile and handed Danny his glass of punch, widening her smile until both rows of pearly white teeth showed.

Sherry, the brunette, didn't even bother to acknowledge them. She had eyes only for Danny. "Dibs on Danny for the next reggae number," she joked in a little-girl voice.

"Dibs on Danny for the next slow dance," Tina countered.

"Now, girls," Danny said, smiling. "No arguments, please. Everybody will get a turn."

The two girls laughed as if it was the funniest thing they had ever heard in their lives.

Melissa saw Lauren give her a wry glance and roll her eyes.

"Danny!" Danny, Melissa, and Lauren looked up and saw B.W. Gonzales leading a group of people in their direction. "These people wanted to meet you."

The group, mostly girls, surrounded Danny, and several programs were shoved in his hands. "Will you sign my program?" asked a wide-eyed girl.

"Mine, too."

"Danny," Tina said, pouting. "The music is starting."

"Give me two minutes," B.W. begged. "I wanted to talk to you about your hosting the rest of the lecture series. Interested?"

Danny cocked his head and pulled the corners of his mouth down as if he were doing B.W. a big favor by considering the question. "Maybe," he answered finally. "Tell me more about it."

"Danny," Melissa called. "Can I talk to you a second?"

"Can't it wait?" he asked impatiently. "I'm kind of busy here."

Melissa fell back, her face flushed with embarrassment, while Danny turned his attention back to B.W.

B.W. launched into an enthusiastic description of the speakers scheduled for the rest of the semester while Danny listened and signed programs.

"Something tells me Danny's not going to have time to punch up our material this evening," Lauren commented.

"All he needs is a cellular phone and a cigar," Melissa said sourly. "Doesn't he realize how obnoxious he's acting?"

"Don't feel bad," Lauren said, putting a hand on Melissa's shoulder. "It's what you wanted for him, isn't it? Healthy self-esteem and all that."

"Healthy self-esteem? Yes. Egomania? No. I think I created a monster. Come on. Let's get out of here."

Abruptly, Melissa turned away. If Danny wanted to talk to her, he knew where to find her. But if he *did* want to talk to her, she thought furiously, he'd better start with the words *I'm sorry.*

Thirteen

KC peered out the bus window at the deserted sidewalks. It was early Saturday morning and none of the shops were open yet. She smothered a yawn and rubbed her eyes. She had skipped the dance and gone to bed early last night because she knew she was going to have to be up early. But she had had a hard time sleeping. She kept dreaming about Brooks. Then her blood would begin to boil and her teeth would clench so tight, the pain in her jaw would wake her up.

The only thing that calmed her down enough to fall back asleep was thinking about the hike she hoped to take with Cody. That would give them an opportunity to talk and straighten things out.

He wanted to get back together. KC was sure of it.

She glanced at her watch. So far, so good. She was right on time.

She had arranged to meet Mr. Hindemann at Mountain Supply, pick up the stuff for the Nature Twins interview, and then meet Cody, Dash, and Lauren at Mount Crinsley.

There was no rain yet, and it was too early to tell which way the weather was going to go. KC crossed her fingers and hoped the rain would hold off. It was called the Rain or Shine Picnic, but she knew that if it rained, they wouldn't be able to count on as big a turnout. Only the true campus eccentrics would show up for a picnic in bad weather.

None of the shops were open yet, but the diner on the corner was, and KC saw a few students going in for an early breakfast. She noted with satisfaction that they all had Mountain Supply umbrellas under their arms.

The bus came to a stop with a creak and KC jumped to her feet. The bus driver gave her a friendly nod as she descended the steps.

There was a whoosh and a roar behind her as the bus pulled back out into the street. KC's hiking boots quickened their steps. She had on her khaki pants and green cable-knit sweater again. It was a perfect outfit for a hike, and the pants showed off her slim waist and long legs. Her long dark hair was pushed back with a black headband.

Mr. Hindemann was waiting outside the shop and waved as she hurried up the sidewalk. Then he actually smiled. "I just sold the last two umbrellas I was planning to keep for myself," he announced. "Couple of kids saw me standing here and begged me to sell them so they could be in the video. That umbrella idea was a good one, KC. It brought lots of people in. Some of them wound up spending serious money."

KC smiled. "Great. I'm glad it worked out for you."

"This is going to be the best spring season we've had in a long time. I give you full credit. Your trial period is up, and I'm satisfied." He held out his hand, and KC shook it. "I think you can count on working here as long as you want. Come on in. I've got the stuff for the interview all boxed up. You'd better take my car."

KC's heart lifted as she followed Mr. Hindemann into the store. Her problems with the phone company were over. She'd earn the money she owed them in no time.

Take that, Brooks Baldwin. She felt her mouth tighten in a grim smile. Brooks had launched an all-out campaign to destroy her, and he'd failed. She had used hard work, persistence, and intelligence to overcome Mr. Hindemann's misgivings about her.

Now it was time to concentrate her attention on Cody. Hard work, persistence, and intelligence were going to pay off there, too.

Now, if Winnie would just keep the promise KC had extracted from her last night and call the housing office about making some new housing arrangements—they could all count on a happy ending to the day.

"This is it, folks. The last event of Bumbershoot. This is Cody Wainwright, broadcasting from Mount Crinsley. Believe it or not, there's no rain right now—but if you're planning to come out, bring your Mountain Supply umbrella anyway so you can be in the video. In just a little while, we're going to be talking to Alice and Gustav Mulch, also known as the Nature Twins, and . . ."

Winnie sat straight up and shrieked. "Oh, no! I overslept again!"

She jumped to her feet and kicked the sleeping bag out of her way. Then she brought her hand down over the top of the clock radio, tapping the button and shutting Cody off. She had arranged to meet Stephanie at Mount Crinsley more than ten minutes ago.

Winnie peeled off the ankle-length T-shirt she used as a nightgown and practically leaped into her black spandex tights and long black sweater. It lacked imagination, but Winnie didn't have time to think about her clothes this morning. She reached for a belt that hung over the desk chair and began winding it around her waist as she scurried around the room, getting her things together.

Stephanie needed her.

Not only that, she had absolutely sworn to KC—sworn on her sacred honor, cross her heart and hope to die—that she would telephone the housing office today and at least go on record as requesting help in finding someplace to live.

Winnie pawed around in the bottom of her carry-all until her fingers closed over a coin. Bingo. A quarter! On her first try, too.

This had to mean something. This had to mean her luck was about to change. Winnie ran barefoot out into the hall to call before she lost her nerve.

She dropped the quarter into the phone and dialed the housing-office number. After two rings, there was a series of whirs and clicks, and then . . .

"Thank you for calling the University of Springfield Housing Office. We no longer keep office hours on Saturdays and Sundays, but if you will leave your name, number, reason for your call, and a time when you can be reached, we will return your call at the earliest possible opportunity."

Beep!

Winnie took a deep breath. "Hi. This is Winnie Gottlieb-Gaffey. Soon to be just Winnie

Gottlieb again because I'm probably going to be getting a divorce which is sort of why I'm calling you. It probably doesn't matter because your records probably just say Winnie Gottlieb and not Gottlieb-Gaffey since after I got married I moved off campus and I wasn't your problem anymore. But I'm your problem again now. Actually, I'm KC's problem but she'd like for me to be your problem so please call me . . . because I need a place to live," she blurted out in panic just as the machine at the other end of the line went . . .

Beep!

Winnie broke off and stared mournfully at the telephone. There were a lot of things she loved about the twentieth century: airplanes, electric guitars, penicillin, mousse.

But answering machines were definitely not on the list. There was simply no way to get her thoughts organized, articulated, and down on tape in twenty seconds. It just couldn't be done. There was no point in trying. She would go by the housing office on Monday morning and speak to somebody in person.

But at least when KC asked her if she had called, she wouldn't have to lie. She could truthfully say that she had called the housing office about getting a room.

The floor was getting cold under Winnie's feet, and the big toe on each foot was numb. It was time to find socks, boots, and her Mountain

Supply umbrella and get to Mount Crinsley.

She turned around and . . .

"Argh!" she screamed in startled surprise.

Marielle was standing right behind her, her eyes slightly glazed. "Surprise!" she slurred. Then she threw back her head and laughed.

Winnie smiled thinly. "That's very entertaining, Marielle. Thank you."

But Marielle wasn't through. She put her hand on Winnie's sleeve and tugged. "Don't run off yet," she said, giggling. "Tell Marielle what the housing office said. Is KC going to get a demerit for letting you share her room?"

Winnie began to back away. Marielle gave her the creeps. Totally.

Marielle let out a high-pitched, hysterical peal of laughter and slapped her thigh. "This story just gets better and better. Wait until I tell Christine Van Diem."

Winnie frowned. "What does Christine Van Diem care?" she asked. Boy! Marielle was really out in the ozone this morning.

"Don't you know?" Marielle was laughing so hard, Winnie had a hard time getting the words. "Christine is Angela Beth Whitman's best friend. Lucky thing she's got such a big mouth—otherwise Angela Beth might not have found out about your illegal living situation. And I might not have found out that Angela Beth is behind this whole thing."

"What whole thing?"

Marielle leaned against the wall and doubled over. "The plot to get KC."

"What are you talking about?" Winnie whispered. Marielle was zonked. Too zonked to realize she was spilling some top-secret beans.

"You dummy. Don't you get it? Angela Beth has Brooks wrapped around her little finger. She pressured Brooks into turning KC in for the phone scam. Then she tried to get him to tell KC's boss the dirt. Brooks wouldn't do it, though. That made little Princess Angela Beth mad. So she wrote a note to the housing office about KC—even forged Brooks's name at the bottom. Angela Beth told Christine all about it. And Christine told me."

Marielle began laughing so hard, she doubled over again. And this time, she lost her balance, falling heavily to the floor. "Oops," she said, giggling.

Winnie didn't stop to help her up. What she wanted to do was grind her heel into Marielle's stupid, laughing face. How could she laugh like that? KC and Brooks had been friends since high school. Angela Beth's lies and plots had driven a wedge between them.

KC hated Brooks now. She saw him as her archenemy, her nemesis, but she was all wrong. Brooks hadn't turned on KC. He wasn't trying to ruin her life. It was all Angela Beth's work.

Winnie ran into KC's room, grabbed her socks, and pulled them on. She had to get to Mount Crinsley. Stephanie was waiting for her. And KC needed to know what was really going on before she ran into Brooks and did something awful.

Fourteen

KC felt Faith tug the arm of her sweater and then gently move her a few inches to one side so that Ted could shift the position of his video camera a bit.

They were standing at the side of the makeshift wooden stage that had been constructed at the Mount Crinsley picnic grounds. Cody stood at the mike with Dash and Lauren. Behind them was a five-piece bluegrass band that had been hired to play for the Rain or Shine Picnic.

The Nature Twins interview was coming to its close, and it had been a huge success. Alice and Gustav Mulch had given lots of silly advice about sports, camping, and nature. The bit had been very funny, full of puns and double entendres.

The clothes and camping equipment had really perked up the sketch, and they had started getting laughs the second they appeared on stage. Lauren wore a flannel shirt and a life vest. A red hunting cap covered her fine blond hair, and the visor rested on the top of her wire-rim glasses. A fishing pole was balanced over her shoulder like a rifle, and every once in a while she would point the pole toward the sky like a hunter and pretend to fire. Dash wore red long underwear and overalls. On his head was a straw farmer's hat, and on his feet, snow skis. The huge crowd burst into laughter and applause as Lauren delivered the last line and the drummer hit the snare, indicating that the bit was over. Cody grinned and began thanking the Nature Twins as the bluegrass band began to play.

Lauren and Dash took their bows and then shuffled off the stage. Cody lifted his hands and applauded in their direction for a few moments, then he faced the audience. "Let's see the umbrellas!" he shouted.

Ted moved to the center of the stage and turned the video camera on the audience as umbrella after umbrella opened up and revealed the words "MOUNTAIN SUPPLY."

It made for a pretty impressive visual effect. Soon the crowd looked as if it were hidden beneath a huge tent. The rocky, snowcapped mountain and the thick clumps of pines created an incredible background. KC's mind immediately began picturing posters of the shot. It would make a great giveaway item for Mountain Supply.

"Get one long shot of that and then cut back to the band," Cody instructed Ted in an undertone. He turned to face her. "KC, Ted's going to tape the band for a couple of numbers, then we'll get you back up here on the stage and you'll do the 'Nature Twins were brought to you by Mountain Supply' pitch. And . . ." he said, grinning at Faith, ". . . th—th—th—that's all, folks."

KC began walking down the wooden steps on the side of the stage with Cody behind her. A knot of people had gathered around Dash and Lauren to congratulate them. KC could see that it would be a while before she could speak with them. That was fine. It meant that Cody and she would have a few moments to themselves.

"Cody," she began, turning to face him.

But to her surprise, Cody wasn't behind her. He was several yards away, walking toward Joel and Dahlia, who were waiting beneath the shade of a large tree. Joel was dressed in his baby-media-executive outfit—jeans, white shirt, tie. Dahlia had on some kind of hippie dress that looked like an Indian-print bedspread that had been through the laundry one time too many. Faded purple and salmon color. It was practically transparent, and had a strange, shrunken hem that barely cleared her round-toed, grungy boots. *Yuck!* KC thought.

Joel clapped Cody on the shoulder, said something, then hurried off, leaving Dahlia and Cody alone under the tree.

As KC watched, Cody stepped closer to Dahlia. There was a lazy, flirtatious smile on his face. Dahlia smiled back, her vague expression turning warm and fuzzy. They exchanged a few words, then Cody put his arms around her waist and bent his head down to kiss her lips.

KC's ears suddenly felt as if they were on fire, and her fingers felt like ice. Her hands flew to her face in horror. This was a dream or something. She couldn't really be seeing what she was seeing.

It wasn't possible. Cody was crazy about her. *Wasn't he?*

Cody and Dahlia must have sensed that they were being watched, because they both turned in her direction at the same time. The smile left Cody's face as his eyes met KC's.

She longed to look away. To run. To pretend that she hadn't seen. Or at least pretend that she didn't care. But she couldn't. Her lips were trembling and she could feel her eyes growing larger.

Cody said something to Dahlia and let go of her waist. Dahlia's arms reluctantly slid from his neck, her hands trailing along his shoulders and down his arms as she released him.

He was walking toward KC now. Walking toward her with an easy, unhurried gait. How dare he look so at ease? How dare he look so self-confident?

Heartbreak gave way to rage as her anger and disappointment bubbled over. "You jerk!" she hissed at him through gritted teeth as soon as he was within earshot.

Cody recoiled and his eyebrows flew up in surprise. "What's the matter with you?" he asked.

"What's the matter?" she practically shouted. "Couldn't you at least have waited until I wasn't looking? How can you cheat on me and rub it in my face like that?"

"Cheat on you?" he repeated in a stunned voice. "*Cheat?* KC! We're over. I thought we were straight on that. Didn't we agree that we were going to be friends?"

"Friends, huh?" she choked.

Hot tears were rolling down her cheeks. Cody's face was a study in helpless, unhappy confusion. "Yes. Friends," Cody repeated. "You agreed. I mean, I thought you agreed. Please believe I never meant to hurt you."

"If you just wanted to be *friends,* why did you come to the store and do such a big job of selling me to Hindemann?" she demanded.

"Because you are my friend," he said softly. He reached into his back pocket and produced a bandanna. Gently, and with great tenderness, he began to wipe the tears from her cheeks. "I wanted to see you do well. I wanted to help you."

KC's eyes searched Cody's for some glimmer of love, of passion. "But you came to my dorm," she argued.

"To see Dahlia," he reminded her sadly.

KC's shoulders shook and her teeth were chattering. "You felt something. I know you did. When Marielle pushed us together, I know you felt what I felt."

Cody turned her face upward and KC's eyes searched his for some sign that he still cared for her the way she cared for him. But all she saw in his eyes was distant affection. And pity.

"KC," he said in his slow, Tennessee drawl. "You're a beautiful girl and you will always make my heart beat faster. But the long and the short of it is this . . . I don't trust you."

KC made a little cry of protest, but Cody released her chin, folded the bandanna, and put it back in his pocket. "I don't trust you to tell me the truth about yourself and about what you're feeling. I don't trust you not to jump to unflattering conclusions about me, and then act on them. I don't trust you not to hurt me."

Before KC could say another word, Faith came hurrying toward them. "KC," she said breathlessly. "You're on in two minutes."

Cody and KC both nodded at Faith, and then she was gone. A blur of blue denim, blond braid, and flashing silver earrings. KC watched her race back up to the stage and whisper something to Ted.

"You'd better get going," KC heard Cody say quietly. His hand pressed against her back, pushing her in the direction of the stage.

KC nodded and blinked her eyes, fiercely willing away the tears, trying desperately to pull herself together. The crowd became quiet as she stepped up to the stage and walked over to the microphone. "On behalf of Mountain Supply," she said, launching into the short spiel she had committed to memory, "I would like to thank you all for being here today."

She finished the pitch on automatic pilot, hardly even aware of what she was saying. Suddenly her eyes focused on a familiar face in the front row.

Brooks!

He was standing next to Angela Beth and staring off into space with the same vacant, confused expression she had seen on his face the day he walked into Mountain Supply. The day he had confessed to her that *he* was the one responsible for this whole series of disasters.

How dare he stand there watching her after ruining her life? After informing on her to the phone company. After trying to get her fired. After writing a letter to the housing office reporting Winnie's illegal presence.

After causing Cody to break up with her!

KC's anger was so huge and so hot, she felt as if her chest were going to explode. It was time to start fighting back, time to let the world know exactly who it was that was ruining her life. "I'd like to add a personal message," she said quickly, hearing the band begin to strike up a tune behind her. "Something I think you should all know." The guitar petered out and the fiddle trailed off.

The quiet audience became even quieter as KC pointed an accusing finger at Brooks. "Brooks Baldwin has been trying to destroy me. He's a low-down, back-stabbing weasel. A coward. An informer. I'm putting him on notice—and you're all witnesses. I'm fighting back," she spat. "What goes around comes around. You ruined my life, Brooks. Now my advice to you is watch *your* back." The audience erupted into surprised murmurs and excited chatter as she ran from the stage in tears. The bandleader gestured frantically for the musicians to start playing.

KC caught a glimpse of Faith's stunned face as she hurried away toward the parking lot with tears streaming down her face.

What she had just done was crazy. Absolutely nuts. But who could blame her? Brooks was driving her insane.

Winnie wandered through the milling crowd, running her fingers nervously through her spiky hair and searching for Stephanie, KC, Ted, Faith, or anybody else she knew. She had managed to catch a ride with a girl from KC's dorm, but they had arrived so late that Winnie had missed the Nature Twins interview and the music.

Several students were setting up picnics. The sun was out and the area was relatively dry. It was pretty chilly, though. On the drive up, Winnie had spotted lots of patches of ice and snow along the higher climbing trails.

"Winnie!"

Winnie whirled around and saw Stephanie running toward her wearing thick corduroy pants, a bulky sweater pulled over a white T-shirt, and heavy hiking boots. Her long blond hair was pulled back in a ponytail and her face looked pale and harried. "I just got here a few minutes ago," she exclaimed, grabbing Winnie's hand. "I'm really sorry if you were waiting for me. But I had to wait and sneak out when my folks weren't looking. They were going to pick up our lawyer and then come back to the house to get me so we could all go to the police station together. As soon as they left, I split and headed over here."

Winnie squeezed her hand. "No problem. I just got here myself." She looked around. "Anything going on, or did we miss it all? Have you seen KC?"

"I saw Faith for just a second when I got here. She said she and Ted and KC were leaving to hike. I told them I had to wait for you. I don't know which trail they took."

"Darn!" Winnie exclaimed. "I had something I really wanted to tell KC."

"You can tell her when they get back," Stephanie said. She shrugged and sighed. "It's too bad we won't get to hike." She pointed toward a picnic table. "Let's sit over there and wait for them."

"Hold it!" Winnie cried, twisting her hand so that her fingers now clasped Stephanie's. If KC had already left with Faith and Ted, Winnie would have to wait to tell her the truth about Brooks. In the meantime, it was important that she and Stephanie establish a little independence.

"What?"

"We don't have to wait for them. Why don't we take a hike on our own?"

"You mean by ourselves?" Stephanie asked skeptically. "That might not be such a good idea."

"We've got to start thinking more positive thoughts. No wonder we have such crummy self-esteem. We think we can't do anything on our own."

"But we don't know the trails or anything."

"Neither do they," Winnie pointed out. "So why are we so willing to trust them? Let's put our trust in us this time. We've come this far under our own steam. Let's not stop now. Let's go hiking on our own." She grinned. "Then we can make up all kinds of stuff to brag about later—like telling them we saw Big Foot or something." Winnie gave Stephanie a playful push in the direction of a rocky path that led up the side of Mount Crinsley.

Stephanie began to giggle, taking long strides to compensate for the suddenly steep incline. "Or the Abominable Snowman."

Winnie matched her strides to Stephanie's. "Or the Loch Ness Monster."

"He's in Scotland."

"Who says the Loch Ness Monster is a *he*?" Winnie said. "Maybe it's a *she*. And maybe she got sick of hanging out in some lake in Scotland and decided to move to Springfield and live in a nice cave on Mount Crinsley."

Stephanie laughed. The path turned and twisted and it wasn't long before the two girls found themselves navigating some icy terrain. "Wow," Stephanie breathed as they turned a corner and caught a glimpse of a meadow spreading out around them. A bluff separated their hiking trail from the meadow. "This is like a postcard. There's even ice along the paths and stuff. And look at all those trees."

"It doesn't take long to get lost in the scenery," Winnie agreed. "And these are the low trails. If you go higher up, above the tree line, you wouldn't believe how icy it is. Not that I've been up there myself," she added. "But that's what I'm told." She frowned and looked around. "You know, I haven't seen anybody around this path since we left. I wonder if we ought to think about going back."

Stephanie stepped forward out on a ledge to get a better look around, then shrieked as the ledge gave way and crumbled beneath her.

"Stephanie!" Winnie jumped back and screamed as Stephanie disappeared from view, falling down into a bluff.

There was a long silence, and Winnie held her breath. "Stephanie," she called again, her voice trembling. She'd heard stories about accidents on Mount Crinsley—people who fell and were never seen again.

"Stephanie?" she cried again in a hoarse whisper. She stepped cautiously forward, terrified of what she might see.

Her hands and legs were trembling so much she could hardly stand. As she leaned out over the ledge, her eyes were squinched shut, and her imagination was cranking into high gear.

Slowly she opened one eye, then let out a sigh of relief. Stephanie lay sprawled on a ledge only a few feet below Winnie. And she was moving, slowly getting up on her knees and shaking her head. "Winnie?" she called.

"I'm here," Winnie cried. "Right above you."

Stephanie turned her face upward and Winnie saw that her face was scraped and bleeding. Still, she didn't seem to be too badly hurt. She was on her feet now and her stunned, confused face was looking for some way to get back up the side of the mountain.

She put her hands on the side of the slanting mountain wall that led up to Winnie's level and felt around for handholds. But the rocky wall was sheer and covered with ice.

"I think I may be stuck down here," Stephanie muttered. She hadn't fallen far, but she was too far below Winnie for Winnie to be able to extend her hand and hoist her up.

Winnie looked right and left, hoping to spot some sign of life, somebody that might know what to do in a case like this. "Hello!" she yelled. "Can anybody hear me?"

Her voice rang out, echoing slightly. But there was no answering call. "HELP!" she screamed again at the top of her lungs. But the note of panic she heard in her voice set off jangling alarm bells in her brain and frightened her even more. She shut her mouth with a snap and fought the temptation to give in to hysterics.

"There's nobody around," Stephanie whimpered fearfully. "And I'm stuck down here."

Right on cue, the edge of the ledge on which Stephanie stood began to crumble, sending a flurry of dirt, ice, and rocks tumbling down the side of the mountain. Stephanie gasped and threw herself forward toward the rocky wall until the mini avalanche finished.

Winnie stifled the impulse to start screaming bloody murder. She forced herself to take some deep breaths. *Calm down,* she ordered herself sternly. There had to be some way of rescuing Stephanie. There just had to be.

Fifteen

Brooks carefully lifted his foot, rested it on the outcropping, then slowly leaned into it, testing its strength. The outcropping held, and Brooks transferred his other foot from the rocky divot in the wall to the outcropping, balancing all his weight on it.

He took some deep breaths, then reached up, grappling with the rocky mountainside in search of a handhold. His toe began sliding out and upward, in search of a toehold.

He had left the walking trail and decided to climb. He was high up on the mountain, above the tree line. But he wasn't high enough yet. The climb wasn't tough enough.

What he really wanted was a climb so tough, so challenging, and so dangerous that he wouldn't be able to think about anything else.

Not have to think about KC. Not have to feel the humiliation of being denounced as a traitor in front of the whole campus. And not have to feel like Angela Beth's stooge.

He felt so awful, he groaned out loud. Maybe he should just throw himself off a cliff and be done with it. Life was just way too confusing for him. Too full of contradictory messages. Too full of emotional land mines. Every step he took was wrong. Life kept blowing up in his face.

"Brooks," he heard Angela Beth call out. "You're going too fast."

"Leave me alone," he begged through gritted teeth. Why had she insisted on coming with him? He didn't want her around. Didn't want to have to listen to her.

"You're taking this way too seriously. Nobody cares what KC thinks or says."

"Please go back to the picnic grounds," he grunted, using all his upper-body strength to hoist himself up on a ledge. He lifted a leg, threw it over the top, then pulled the rest of his body up.

Slowly he stood, looking out over the valley below and panting for breath. He was higher up than he had thought.

He fought a little for breath. The air was thin up here. He tried breathing deeply, counting his breaths as he inhaled and exhaled. He looked out, enjoying the aerial view from high up on Mount Crinsley. He began to feel better.

It was icy. Too icy to be climbing without equipment. But maybe it was a better and more challenging test of his skills and ability and *courage* this way.

Far below him, he saw the rooftops of Springfield and the old logging trails that criss-crossed the landscape. He kicked his toe against a partly glaciated area of rock and wished he were alone.

A man could think up here.

A man could find himself up here.

A man could come up with some answers up here.

If a man could get a few minutes of peace and quiet.

He saw Angela Beth's hands grip the edge of the ledge and she began to try to hoist herself up. For an insane moment, he almost considered stepping on her fingers.

Brooks forced himself to take a step back. Was he losing his mind? He raked his fingers down the side of his face, clawing at his cheeks. He did feel as though his grip on reality was slipping. Every time he got his feelings into focus, Angela Beth came along and turned everything upside down for him—her touch, her voice, her logic—she was like some kind of sorceress, and he was afraid of her now. Afraid of what she might make him do.

Her leg came up and hooked on the edge of the ledge. The dark ponytail appeared first, then slowly, the rest of her body began to emerge. Angela Beth was amazingly strong. Amazingly athletic. It was almost supernatural.

He took another fearful step back as she climbed to her feet and faced him, efficiently tightening the ponytail. "What's the matter with you?" she demanded. "What happened to the Brooks Baldwin I used to know? The Brooks Baldwin who knew right from wrong?"

"Leave me alone!" he bellowed.

"If you were a real man," she hissed, "you wouldn't be out here trying to get away from me. You would be helping me see that KC Angeletti and her friends don't get away with making you, me, the Gammas, and everybody else look bad." She took a step closer, and Brooks retreated until his back was against the rocky side of the mountain.

Her face was close to his now, and he could feel her breath on his cheek. "I need you to help me, Brooks."

"What is it now?" he asked hoarsely. Anger, anxiety, and desire were making him feel dizzy, queasy, and faint.

A slow smile creased Angela Beth's face. "You weren't at the ODT party the night Stephanie got herself into trouble. But people know you and trust you, Brooks. If *you* said you were there, and that the rape charge against Christopher is a setup—people would believe you."

"NO!" he roared, lifting his hands to push her back. "I won't lie for you! And you can't make me!" His hands hovered over her shoulders, itching to grab her lithe body and throw it over the side.

Instead, he turned abruptly, scanned the rock face that soared above him, and leaped in the air, grabbing the rocky outcropping that protruded several feet over his head. Then he swung his body toward the icy cliff wall. "I'm going to the top. Don't try to follow me."

"Brooks!" Angela Beth called out. "Wait. It's too dangerous. Don't go up the side any farther. Take the path."

"Go away and leave me alone," he begged. He was crying now. All he wanted was peace and quiet to be able to think things through, and try to figure out how and why he and KC had become such bitter enemies. "Don't follow me," he ordered again. "Don't even speak to me. Ever again."

"Forget about it," Ted said. "I'll clip the last couple of minutes off the end of the video. Believe me, people have short memories. By this time tomorrow, nobody will remember what you said to Brooks."

"I don't want them to forget," KC choked. She pulled at the neck of her sweater as if she were stretching it to give herself more room. Then she pulled another tissue from the pocket of her khakis and dabbed at her nose. "I want everybody to know what a skunk he is."

Ted shot a look at Faith. Faith plucked unhappily at one of her silver earrings and twitched her blond braid off the shoulder of her denim jacket. She lowered her eyes, as if she were working hard to think of some comforting words for KC.

As soon as KC had come charging off the stage in tears, Faith had taken off after her. Ted had had to get the video camera stowed in the trunk of Hindemann's car. By the time he had caught up with them, KC had calmed down some. But she was still pretty upset.

The three of them were walking along the lower paths, trying to get a little distance from the crowd and comfort KC. Faith put her arm around KC's shoulder. "It'll be okay," she said in a low voice. "You'll see. We'll all spend the evening together and . . ."

KC twisted out from under Faith's arm. "No—it won't be okay," she said evenly. "Nothing will ever be okay again." Her lips trembled. "I think I need to be alone for a little while," she whispered. "Excuse me."

"KC," Faith cried as KC began running back down the path. "Wait!"

She started to run after her, but Ted reached out and grabbed her hand. "Don't," he said.

Faith's blue eyes were large with worry and concern. "Ted, I don't want her to be alone right now. She—"

"She wants to be alone," Ted said in an insistent voice. "So give her some space and some time."

Faith's mouth fell open. "You make it sound like I'm some kind of meddler," she said in disbelief. "I'm her friend."

"Then respect her wishes," Ted said firmly. "And face reality. You're not a therapist, you're not a priest, you're not a psychiatrist. You've got to quit taking the weight of everybody's problems on your own shoulders."

Faith looked so shocked and hurt that he immediately regretted his harsh words. "I'm sorry," he said quietly. "I'm just so frustrated by this situation, I can't help exploding. And it's not KC I'm upset about. It's Stephanie. Faith, you've got to tell Stephanie to get some professional help. She's got to get over depending on you and me to meet her extremely complicated emotional needs. We can't do it. I know I can't. And if you would get honest about it, you'd know you can't, either."

Faith's face looked frozen.

Ted wiped his mouth with the back of his hand, then stood with his hands on his hips, staring off at the mountains for a moment. Debating.

Did he want to gamble everything?

He had nothing left to lose, he decided. There was almost nothing left of their old relationship. It was definitely ultimatum time. "Tell her to get professional help, or you and I are through." He worked hard to keep his tone of voice as neutral as possible. "I'm sorry to put it on that basis. But I don't feel like I have any choice anymore."

Faith turned and stared out at the mountains too. Her mouth quivered and her long lashes fluttered. Then her face crumpled and her hands flew to her mouth, stifling a miserable wail.

Ted put his arms around her, feeling like a dog. He didn't take the ultimatum back, though. He meant it. He really did.

"You're right," she sobbed into his shoulder. "I know you're right. I've known it for a long time."

"Then why keep butting your head against a wall?" he asked in genuine confusion. "I don't get it. Why give me up over a problem you know you can't solve?"

"Because I can't face telling Stephanie that she can't depend on me," Faith admitted. "On us. I can't face the guilt I know I'm going to feel. We're the ones who encouraged her to press charges against Christopher. We promised we'd be there for her no matter what. How can we back out now?"

Ted pulled her hands from her face and led her

over to a fallen tree trunk. "I'm not talking about cutting her out of our lives completely." He sat her down on the trunk and took a seat next to her, draping an arm around her shoulder. "I'm talking about encouraging her to find her own resources. I'm talking about drawing some boundaries."

Faith nodded wearily and pulled a tissue from her pocket. "Okay. You're right. I'll tell her."

"I'll tell her if you can't face it," Ted offered.

"No!" Faith shook her head. "I'll tell her. I'll draw the line." She leaned her head against Ted's shoulder. "I'm not looking forward to it, though."

Sixteen

Winnie spiked up her hair for luck before creeping slowly to the edge of the icy overhang, the length of her belt looped over her arm like a rope. Fortunately it was one of those long, braided leather jobs that wrapped around her waist three or four times.

"Catch the end when I lower it," she ordered Stephanie. "And rub your hands in the dirt so they don't slip when you pull it," she added.

Stephanie nodded and leaned over, rubbing her palms in the dirt as Winnie lowered the belt. Then she straightened and watched as Winnie carefully positioned herself so that she was lying on her stomach, one end of the belt tied firmly around her waist.

"Hold it," Stephanie said. "That's not going to work. I'm going to wind up pulling you down here."

"Not to worry," Winnie said. "I've got my toes dug down between two rocks. That will anchor me."

Stephanie shook her head. "No it won't. I'm just as heavy as you are. Maybe heavier. And you're tilted in this direction."

Winnie wriggled her toes, testing the rigidity of her toehold. There was a lot of room for movement, which meant that her feet weren't as tightly braced as she thought. Stephanie was right. She would wind up slipping down.

"Let me think about this a second," Winnie said.

There was a scuffling, creaking sound as the ledge on which Stephanie stood began to crumble. Stephanie let out a little yip of alarm and reached forward, grasping at some foliage that sprouted from a crack in the rocky wall. "Don't think about it too long," she squeaked.

Winnie rolled over on her back and examined what was left of a gnarled, dead tree trunk that stuck out from the mountainside just above her head. "I think I've got an idea," she said.

Standing up, Winnie fished up the belt and threw it over the tree trunk, close to the root.

"Give it a tug," she ordered as she lowered it again toward Stephanie.

Stephanie jumped carefully and grabbed the end of the belt. Winnie felt a sudden jerk at her waist and leaned her body all the way back. The tree trunk never budged.

"We're okay," Winnie yelled. "Now start climbing." If she turned her head and looked out the corner of her eye, she could see Stephanie as she planted her feet on the slippery incline, using the belt as a climbing rope.

"You're doing great," Winnie yelled.

Stephanie grunted as she struggled to climb, pulling herself hand over hand up the few feet that led to Winnie's level. Her feet skittered for a moment against the ice. "I can't," Stephanie whimpered.

"Yes you can," Winnie urged, leaning even farther back and doing her best to yank Stephanie up a few inches. "Now try it."

Stephanie stomped her feet against the side, managed to plant them, and then in a few quick movements, climbed the wall.

Winnie dropped to the ground and reached forward, grabbing Stephanie by the back of her sweater and pulling her, willy-nilly, up over the side.

"YEOWWW!" both girls cried as they went rolling backward toward safety.

Winnie immediately loosened the belt around

her waist and jumped up, clapping her hands in the air as if she were high-fiving herself. "All right!"

She reached over, pulled Stephanie's arm up, and high fived her. "Thank-*que*! Thank-*que*!" she yelled like a rock star, happily bouncing on her toes and bowing toward an imaginary audience.

Stephanie lay on her back, panting with relief. "What are you doing?" she asked. "I almost got killed, and you're dancing around like you just won first place on *Star Search*."

Winnie pulled her to her feet. "This is better than winning first place on *Star Search*. Don't you see? We got into a terrible jam. And all by ourselves we got out of it. I don't know about you, but I just felt a big infusion of self-esteem."

Stephanie's pale and shaken face began to relax. "You're right," she said in an incredulous voice. "We helped ourselves."

"Come on," Winnie urged eagerly, wrapping her belt back around her waist. "Let's go back to the picnic grounds and find somebody we know so we can brag."

Stephanie grinned. "Race you," she offered. And with that, she turned and ran.

Twenty minutes later, Faith listened to the story of Stephanie's exciting rescue with wide eyes. She hitched up her jeans and adjusted her silver earrings as she sat down next to Stephanie.

After their own hike, she and Ted had returned to the picnic grounds and spread out the food that Faith had brought. KC had borrowed a big waterproof tarp from Mountain Supply, and they were using it as their picnic blanket.

KC was still off by herself somewhere, but Faith had put aside a roast-beef sandwich for her because she knew it was KC's favorite. The sun was shining now, and the chill in the air was rapidly disappearing. All around them, couples had set up picnics, and several games of Frisbee were in progress. If it weren't for the fact that KC was off somewhere being completely miserable, and Faith was about to have a very unpleasant conversation with Stephanie, it would have been a nice afternoon. At least Dash and Lauren were happy today, she reflected as she took a bite of her tuna-fish sandwich. They were relieved their Nature Twins interview had gone so well, but hadn't been able to stay around and celebrate. They had hitched a ride back to campus with Cody, Dahlia, and Joel. Cody had said he needed to get back to the station. And Lauren and Dash had promised to meet their editor for a last-minute story meeting.

As Winnie babbled happily and snapped the legs of her spandex tights for sound effects, Faith's eyes searched the crowd for Melissa. She hadn't seen her at all today. According to Lauren, Melissa was pretty unhappy with Danny over the way he had behaved at the dance last night. Under the circumstances, she didn't blame Melissa for deciding to skip today's festivities altogether.

". . . and the next thing I knew, Stephanie was lying next to me on the ground," Winnie finished proudly.

Ted put his hand on Stephanie's shoulder. "You guys did great," he said, grinning. He threw Faith a significant look. "I'll bet it makes you feel good to know you can be self-sufficient if you have to be, *doesn't it?*" he finished with emphasis for Faith's benefit.

Faith returned Ted's look with a frown. She was going to talk to Stephanie. He didn't have to push it.

Winnie plunged her hand down into the big paper bag that served as their picnic basket and fished up a sandwich. She handed it to Stephanie and then plunged her hand down again. "You're right. We were talking about that very same thing on the way back, weren't we, Stephanie?"

Faith looked at Stephanie to see how she was reacting. But Stephanie was too busy unwrapping a chicken-salad sandwich to answer. "Looks like that hike gave you an appetite," Faith said. She scootched her bottom slightly closer to her.

"Um hmm." Stephanie nodded absently, taking a hungry bite.

Faith bit her lip. This was going to be tougher

than she thought. It was going to be hard to find the right opening for what she had to say.

Faith caught Ted watching the two of them with an intent expression on his face. She frowned and slightly jerked her head, signifying that this would be easier without him hanging around. She cut her eyes in Winnie's direction too.

Ted nodded, got to his feet, and held his arm out to Winnie. "Come on, Winnie. Bring your sandwich and let's see if we can hunt up a Frisbee."

"Okay by me." Winnie quickly reached in the bag, pulled out another sandwich, and stuffed it into the pocket of her jacket. "For later," she explained, scrambling to her feet while carefully holding up the sandwich in her hand.

As Faith watched, Winnie followed Ted into the crowd and they disappeared. Faith turned back toward Stephanie and caught her staring at her with a speculative look. Stephanie's cheeks suddenly flushed and she dropped her eyes, focusing her attention back on her sandwich.

Faith reached around for her braid and brushed the end back and forth across her lips. It was now or never. And it would be better to tell Stephanie, let her cry it out of her system a little, and be back in control before the others returned. "Steph, I—" she began.

"Faith!" Stephanie said suddenly, cutting her off. "I have to say something and I don't know how."

Small world, Faith thought, her heart sinking. If Stephanie was about to start in with a whole new round of confidences and emotional struggles, Faith would never be able to cut the cord.

But old habits died hard. In spite of her determination to distance herself, she heard her voice automatically responding. "You can tell me anything, Stephanie. You know I'll be here for you."

Stephanie's eyelids closed nervously and then opened again, making her expressive eyes look unnaturally large and vulnerable. "I've been thinking a lot about what happened to me and stuff. And it's really been great being able to talk to you and Ted. But I think maybe I need professional help. Somebody who can help me become more self-reliant."

"What?" Faith breathed.

"Please don't be mad. I mean, I wouldn't ever want you to feel *inadequate* or anything. But if I keep talking to you, I won't take any steps toward helping myself. So would you mind very much if I didn't come by to see you as often?"

Faith's blue eyes crinkled merrily. She bit her lip so she wouldn't burst out laughing. Poor, sweet Stephanie. Worrying that Faith's feelings might be hurt. It was incredibly funny. And incredibly touching.

She took Stephanie's hand and squeezed it. "I think that sounds like a great idea," she said in an encouraging voice. "And even though I'll miss our late-night talks, you know that all I really want is for you to be happy."

Stephanie's face broke into a relieved smile. "Thanks, Faith." Then her face clouded as if she'd suddenly had a disturbing second thought. "You don't think Ted will mind, do you? I wouldn't want him to think I didn't like talking to him or anything like that. He's been great to me too."

"I'm pretty sure it'll be okay." Faith gave Stephanie a conspiratorial wink. "I'll explain it to him very tactfully."

Winnie tossed the Frisbee back to the tall, red-headed girl in the green Army surplus coat. The girl caught it and tossed it toward Ted with an efficient snap of the wrist.

"Nice toss," Ted commented as he lifted his hand and caught it easily. "Heads up, Winnie." He flipped it in Winnie's direction.

She missed the catch and had to turn and chase it as if it were a large, round butterfly. She zigged and zagged in pursuit, then stumbled when she caught a glimpse of a familiar green cable-knit sweater and khaki pants.

KC!

KC was sitting on a rock several yards away, staring off into the distance with a grim look on her face.

The Frisbee hit the ground and bounced twice before Winnie pounced on it. She snatched it up and spun it back to Ted. "I'm out," she announced. "You two carry on."

"Will do!" Ted clicked his heels and saluted just before raising his hand to catch the orbiting saucer. Then he leaned way back, lifted his leg, and tossed the Frisbee underneath his knee toward the redhead.

Winnie giggled, patted her pocket to make sure her spare sandwich hadn't fallen out, and began trotting toward KC. She had a lot of news to tell her.

KC sat with one leg folded underneath her and the other one drawn up under her chin. She continued to stare moodily at a clump of tall trees and didn't stir when Winnie plopped down next to her. "Hi!" Winnie said brightly, pulling at the spikes of her hair so that they pointed toward the sky.

KC grunted and Winnie leaned over and bounced her shoulder against KC's. "Cheer up. I promise I'm moving. I called the housing office today. And I'll go over there Monday."

KC's head nodded a fraction and she grunted again.

"I also had an interesting talk with Marielle Danner. Turns out it's not Brooks who's out to get you."

KC's head snapped toward Winnie. "What?"

"It's Angela Beth," Winnie announced. "And it's been Angela Beth all along."

It wasn't easy for Winnie to tell somebody a complicated story without taking a dozen conversational detours. But this time, she made up her mind to stay on track and convey to KC how Brooks had been manipulated time after time. "According to Marielle . . ." Winnie began.

KC felt the color rapidly draining from her face as Winnie repeated everything Marielle had told her. *I don't trust you not to jump to unflattering conclusions and then act on them. I don't trust you not to hurt me,* Cody had said.

Poor Brooks. She'd done to him what she had done to Cody. And she'd done it twice. She dropped her head in her hands and groaned. Why hadn't she seen it? It had all been so clear. Of course Angela Beth was behind it all.

Brooks was, at heart, one of the most decent men she had ever known. Angela Beth may have bent his resolve here and there, but she hadn't succeeded in changing his essential nature. KC squeezed her eyes shut, remembering how sorry he had been about turning her in. How apologetic. And how accusatory and savage she had been in the Dining Commons.

And on the day that he and Angela Beth had come into Mountain Supply, she should have known he wouldn't tell Hindemann about the phone company. Not after that scene in the Dining Commons. If he had, Hindemann would have fired her on the spot—no ifs, ands, or buts.

On top of that, she hadn't stopped for two minutes to wonder about the note that the housing office had sent her. Why didn't it occur to her that Angela Beth might have written it? Why did she have to go off half-cocked and accuse Brooks of treachery in front of the whole campus?

His stricken, white face floated up in front of her. He'd flinched and recoiled during her speech as if she had been beating him. For somebody like Brooks, she reflected miserably, a beating would have been preferable to a slur on his honor.

She dug her fingers into her cheeks. "Why don't I ever learn?" she groaned deeply.

Winnie shrugged. "You don't have to get that bent out of shape," she chirped. "Just tell Brooks you're sorry about tearing into him. And tell him to tell Angela Beth you've got her number, so she should knock it off already."

"You don't understand," KC protested, guilt and misery making her voice harsh. "After my Mountain Supply announcement, I stood up on the stage, pointed my finger at Brooks, and stated publicly that he was a low-down, back-stabbing weasel."

"KC!"

KC grabbed two big handfuls of her dark hair and pulled hard while drumming her heels against their rocky seat. "Argh! The person I should have been pointing to was Angela Beth. I *humiliated* Brooks for no good reason."

Winnie's fingers tweaked the spikes of her hair, and her brows knitted. "Wow! I wish I'd gotten here sooner. I'm sorry, KC. I'm really sorry."

"It's not your fault," KC said quickly, standing up. "It's mine. And it's time for me to stop blaming my problems on other people. This whole thing would never have started if I hadn't been dishonest and used that phony credit-card number. That's what set this whole thing into motion. I have to take responsibility for that."

Winnie nodded. "You're right about taking responsibility," she said in a small voice. "I'm going to start taking responsibility for things too. And the first thing I'm going to take responsibility for is finding a place to live."

KC reached out and threw her arms around Winnie. "You may be a slob," she whispered, "but I've still liked having you around."

"Really?" Winnie asked happily.

"Really." KC released Winnie's shoulders. "I've got to find Brooks," she said. "I owe him an apology. And the sooner I deliver it, the better."

"Ted said he saw Brooks and Angela Beth starting up the Green trail," Winnie said. "That's for really experienced hikers and climbers. Maybe you should wait until they get back."

KC frowned, looking off at the base of the Green trail. It was a tough hike. But she didn't want to wait one minute longer than necessary to apologize. She lifted her hand and waved. "I'm going hiking," she said with a grin. "And if you hear a scream, it's Angela Beth. I'm really tempted to push her off the mountain."

Brooks sat on a boulder that protruded from the side of the mountain, his head in his hands. He'd succeeded in eluding Angela Beth, but he had lost his heart for climbing and he'd been sitting on this rock for a long time now.

He felt the wind, sharp against his face. He was really high now. Almost to the top. All around him, the mountain was marbled with veins of ice.

But it wouldn't be long before Angela Beth caught up with him. The hiking path took a circuitous route, but eventually it would lead her to where he sat now. He looked down. When you got this high up, the path was really narrow, less than two feet wide. Below it yawned the canyon.

He clapped his hands against his ears as if he could already hear her voice echoing through it. Pleading. Begging. Teasing. Accusing. But no matter what she said, no matter what she did, he wouldn't give in to her. Not again. Not ever again.

"Brooks!" he heard her cry.

"No!" he whispered to himself, tightening his hands against the side of his head. "Don't listen to her. If you start listening, she'll talk you into something."

"Brooks!" the voice called out. More insistent this time and getting closer.

It was no use. No matter how tightly he clamped his hands over his ears, he could still hear her voice.

"Brooks! I want to talk to you." The voice was coming around the bend of the narrow path.

"NO!" Brooks shouted. He jumped up, determined to escape. His eyes quickly scanned the rock face that soared up behind him. There were several handholds and toeholds. But it was also covered with ice and extremely dangerous. Still, if he could get to the top of the mountain, he would be safe. Not even Angela Beth could follow him up this section.

He started up the mountain wall, his fingers and toes finding the crevices in the rocks as if by magic. Brooks smiled. Sometimes climbing was like this; natural, instinctive, as easy as a stroll in the park. He looked down. The narrow ledge that was the path was several feet below him now. And below that was a drop to the very bottom of Mount Crinsley.

"Brooks!" The voice was right below him now. Strange. Angela Beth sounded different in this thin mountain air.

He couldn't help looking down again to see if Angela Beth was watching, fuming as he scurried up the cliff and out of her clutches.

But when he turned, what he saw surprised

him so much, he almost lost his footing and fell.

"Brooks!" KC shrieked as he stumbled to steady himself, digging his fingers into a crevice.

KC! It was KC calling him. Not Angela Beth. What was she doing out here?

He looked down and saw her staring up at him with her hands over her mouth. She looked scared.

Brooks's foot rested on an icy outcropping, and then slipped. He tightened his grasp on the handholds, and quickly searched with his toe for a more reliable toehold. He found it immediately and steadied himself. Then he lifted his hand, feeling along the side of the mountain for something to hold on to.

"Brooks," a second female voice shrieked.

Brooks looked down again. This time it was Angela Beth. "Brooks, come down," she ordered, her voice sharp with alarm. "You're out of your mind to go up there."

Brooks's hand searched and searched. Nothing. He slapped his palm angrily on the side of the mountain. His karma was gone. Kaput. Totally blown.

And no wonder. Between Angela Beth and KC, they were driving him insane. "Leave me alone!" he screamed. "Both of you!"

"Come down, Brooks," KC begged. "Please come down."

"Yes, please come down," Angela Beth echoed,

her imperious voice registering genuine alarm.

They were nuts. Come down for what? To listen to KC rake him over the coals and rip out his guts? To listen to Angela Beth hectoring him about his friends? His manhood? His lost sense of right and wrong?

He wasn't coming down. No way. He was going up.

His hand felt around more urgently, slapping and raking the rocky wall, trying to find something to grab. There had to be a handhold up there. There *had* to be. He'd looked the site over before starting. Mapped it out in his mind. The handhold was there. He'd seen it. And if he could find it, he would be at the top. Safe from Angela Beth. And safe from KC.

It was there—probably just inches higher than his reach. If he jumped, he could probably put his hand on it.

He bent his knees a little, testing the tensile of the outcropping. If he pushed off, he would have to be ready to move on, because the outcropping would be gone. Too much pressure on it and it was sure to break off and crumble away.

"BROOKS!" he heard Angela Beth shout as if she knew what he was planning. "Don't!"

That did it. The shrill, admonishing note in her voice made up his mind for him. He was going for it.

"BROOKS!" he heard KC scream as he pushed off the outcropping. He felt it give way beneath him, and his toes dragged slightly against the rock. His hands scrabbled for the crevice his mind had convinced him was there, and suddenly . . . the insanity of what he had done hit him and he panicked.

His hands clawed wildly . . . but in vain. His feet searched for a perch but couldn't find one. He was sliding. "HELP!" he screamed as his body picked up speed, skating down the side of the cliff and then falling away from it.

"BROOKS!" he heard KC and Angela Beth shriek.

He caught a last glimpse of their faces as he fell past them. Faces that were twisted with horror, mouths open, screaming silently.

Good-bye, his mind said in the poised, composed voice that he recognized as his own. Strange. He was suddenly calm again. Suddenly at peace. There were no more decisions to make. No more risks to calculate. No more women to hurt.

He knew that KC and Angela Beth were still screaming, but he heard nothing. Nothing now but the whooshing sound of the wind as he floated down . . . down . . . down . . .

Seventeen

Melissa sat on her bed, leaning against the wall and looking out the window. She felt drained, depleted, as though if she looked in the mirror, she would discover that the red of her hair and the brown of her freckles had faded to a dusty gray.

Every trace of the rain was gone today, and the sun shone down on the campus and highlighted the mountain peaks.

The sudden sunshine seemed bizarre and inappropriate. How could nature be so cheerful when Brooks, the guy she had once been engaged to marry, had fallen to his death at the age of nineteen?

She had loved him once. Lain in her bed at night and imagined their future together. Then he'd broken their engagement, and she had spent a long time hating him. She realized now that the time she had spent hating him was just another form of loving him. He had been just as present in her thoughts and feelings during their estrangement as he had during their engagement. Now all she could feel was an overwhelming sense of loss, pity, and heartbreak.

"I still can't believe it," Faith said quietly. She sat on Lauren's bed between Dash and Lauren, still wearing the denim blouse, jeans, and silver earrings that she had worn since yesterday. Her red-rimmed blue eyes met Melissa's, and the two girls exchanged a look of deep understanding.

Faith had loved Brooks too. As a girlfriend, and then as a sister. They had known each other almost all their lives, grown up together. Melissa had the feeling that Faith still hadn't fully comprehended the finality of Brooks's death, even though it had been Faith who had come to Melissa's room last night with the news. She had told Melissa what had happened in a straightforward tone of voice. Flat and without emotion. Then she had collapsed on Melissa's shoulder and the two of them had wept for hours.

It had been Faith who had spoken to Brooks's parents this morning on the phone. And it would be Faith who would ride back to their hometown with Brooks's body late this afternoon. Services were scheduled for tomorrow morning.

"Are you sure you don't want us to drive you?" Lauren asked again, raking her fingers through her hair. "Or if you want, Ted can take my Jeep and drive you. You don't want to ride with the people from the funeral home, do you?"

"I'll think about it," Faith said quietly. "Thanks."

There was a soft knock on the door, and Dash jumped up and opened it.

"Hi," Melissa heard a familiar voice say in a subdued tone. "Can I see Melissa?"

Melissa's eye flew toward the door. Danny sat there, staring at her with large, sympathetic eyes. "I just heard," he said. "I was out last night and I didn't hear about Brooks until this morning and . . ." His face flushed and his voice broke. "Can I talk to you?" he said. "Alone?"

"Sure," Melissa responded softly. Her legs felt stiff and achy as she got off the bed and walked into the hallway. Danny shut the door, and Melissa leaned against the wall of the empty hallway with her arms folded over her chest.

"I'm so sorry," he said.

Melissa's lip trembled, and a sob rose in her throat.

"About everything," Danny blurted out. He reached up and pulled at the fingers of one of her hands. "Sit down. Please."

Melissa let him lower her into his lap and pull

her head down on his shoulder. The fabric of his long-sleeved green T-shirt felt soft against her cheek. "I'm sorry about the way I acted. I'm sorry about Brooks. And I'm sorry about every self-pitying, guilt-inducing thing I ever said." He shook his head. "Something like this puts things in perspective real fast. I'm glad to be alive. And I'm glad you're my girlfriend. For the first time in a long time, I'm thinking I'm a lucky guy."

Melissa was sobbing now, pressing her face into the solid muscles of his shoulder for comfort.

"Will you forgive me? Can we start over?"

Melissa didn't answer. She couldn't. It didn't matter now. None of it. Not the bursts of temper, the bouts of ego, or the other girls. She put her arms around his neck and moved her head down so that it lay against his chest. She needed to hear the beating of his heart. Needed the comfort that came with being reminded that he was here, and alive.

Angela Beth's eyes were so irritated from weeping, she could hardly see the faces of her sorority sisters as she looked around the living room of the Gamma house.

Several of the girls were there, keeping her company. There was a hushed, confused, and surreal quality to the scene.

"I still can't believe it," one girl whispered. "What a terrible accident! Did anybody see it besides Angela Beth?"

Angela Beth pressed her handkerchief to her mouth and began to sob again.

"Shh," Christine Van Diem warned the girl. "Don't be so tactless."

Angela Beth couldn't talk. She was too upset. Too heartbroken. And too *enraged*.

But if she could have, she would have told Christine not to silence the questions of the other girls. Of course someone else had seen it. KC Angeletti had been there and seen it all. And the more Angela Beth thought about it, the less like an accident it seemed.

KC might as well have pushed him, she reflected savagely, grinding her white teeth. She as good as murdered him. The whole campus knew she was out to get him. They had seen her lash out at him. Threaten him. And she had been the one to suggest that Brooks try a dangerous climb.

She felt Christine's hand on her back as she bent her head and wept. KC Angeletti had ruined her life and murdered the man she loved. Was there nothing that KC wasn't prepared to do in order to destroy her?

Around her, she heard her sorority sisters discussing the *accident* in low, sibilant voices. Somehow Angela Beth would find a way to make them see that what had happened to Brooks was no accident. That it had a been a murder.

A cold-blooded, premeditated murder.

And the murderess was KC.

*   *   *

KC glanced at herself in the mirror. She looked as though she had aged twenty years since yesterday. She felt as if she were still in shock: numb, shaky, and slightly sick.

The horror of watching Brooks fall to his death was so awful and so overwhelming that she just couldn't think about it. If she did, she knew she would burst into a hysterical screaming fit.

Winnie was out, but KC wished she would come back. They had returned together last night after what had seemed like an eternity spent at Mount Crinsley.

Rescue teams, park rangers, police, and paramedics had flooded the area, and it had taken hours for them to locate and retrieve Brooks's body.

Then there had been questions. *Had he been an experienced climber? Had he climbed that rock before? Had he seemed upset about anything?*

It had been the worst day of KC's whole life. And through it all, Winnie had stayed right beside her, holding her hand and for once being quiet and subdued. When they'd finally gotten home last night, the two of them had sat up practically until dawn. They'd huddled together while KC wept. Finally she had fallen asleep with her head on Winnie's shoulder.

This morning it was as if they had both decided to keep moving so they wouldn't have to think. KC had immediately thrown herself into a manic cleanup. And Winnie had efficiently gathered her papers together and gone off to hunt up a housing office employee even though it was Sunday.

KC picked up a stack of clothes from the floor and dropped them on the chair so she could sweep. Then she picked up the green cable-knit sweater and khakis and bundled them into the wastebasket. She didn't have many clothes, but she never wanted to see that sweater and those pants again. They would only remind her of . . .

She pushed the thought to the back of her mind and reached for the broom.

A glance at the clock told her that Winnie had been gone an hour. She was just wondering what Winnie had been able to work out when the door burst open and Winnie came hurrying in. For once, her clothes looked fairly normal. No bright tights. No weird headgear. No ponyhide boots. Just some jeans, a sweatshirt, and sneakers. "I managed to talk to somebody from the housing office at their home, and here's the scoop," she said breathlessly.

KC pushed aside a stack of folded clothes and sat down on the bed, giving Winnie her attention.

"The housing office will see what they can do about finding me a room ASAP. But under the circumstances, if you want me to stay on and keep you company, they'll give us special permission to room together here."

KC nodded but didn't answer. Winnie sat down on the bed. "Say something, KC. I mean, I know you're totally overwhelmed with grief. We all are. But I need you to let me know what you want."

KC sighed and shook her head. It was hard to think. Hard to focus. Hard to imagine the next few hours, never mind the next few weeks.

"I'm worried about you," Winnie confided, draping her arm around KC's shoulders. "You've taken care of me for a long time. Now it's time for me to return the favor and take care of you. Be here for you. Keep you company."

"Thanks," KC said, grateful for Winnie's loyalty. "Thanks for sticking by me."

"Hey! What are friends for?" Winnie whispered.

KC stared at Winnie's forlorn face and felt a surge of affection. Winnie was heartbroken over Brooks's death. But she was keeping her feelings in check in an effort to comfort KC—who was not only heartbroken, but wracked with guilt, too.

It was all my fault, she thought for about the hundredth time.

"No it wasn't," Winnie argued.

"Huh?" KC put her hand to her face. Was she losing her mind? Had she said it out loud?

"It wasn't your fault," Winnie said forcefully. "I could tell by the look on your face that that's what you were thinking. And that's why I think I ought to stay here with you. Somebody's got to keep you from deciding that you killed Brooks or something like that."

"I don't need company," KC said. "But I appreciate the offer. What I need is for time to go backward," she choked. "I need to go back and make things right—erase this whole feud with Brooks. Forget the whole climb on Mount Crinsley." Her lip trembled. "What I want . . ." she began.

Winnie's eyes searched her face. "What?" she pressed gently.

"What I want . . ." KC tried again. She could hardly get the words out, hardly make herself say it.

"Tell me," Winnie urged.

"What I want is for Brooks to be alive," she wailed. "And for him to be my friend again."

Then she laid her head in Winnie's lap and sobbed.

Here's a sneak preview of
Freshman Suspect, *the thirty-second
book in the compelling story
of* FRESHMAN DORM.

"*M*iss Angeletti, I'm waiting."

KC's eyes blinked open, and she realized that her lips were starting to tremble with emotion. It was hard to talk about the day when Brooks died. Didn't this woman understand? "I couldn't catch up with him on the trail, so I started calling to him," KC pushed on. "I wanted to apologize. But Angela Beth was up ahead of me. And she was calling for him, too. I don't know if he even heard me before he—" KC broke off. She started to cover her eyes with one hand, then dropped it back into her lap. "I've already told the police everything. Why are you questioning me again?"

"How can you be so sure Ms. Whitman was ahead

of you on the trail?" Lieutenant Landau prodded her.

KC looked up sharply. She was falling through space and her heart was pounding, waiting for the fatal impact. "Because I could *see* her." KC's voice began to rise with indignation. "I mean, from time to time she was hidden by rocks and trees, but . . ."

"So you're not sure."

"Yes!" KC finally burst out. "Yes, I'm sure. She was definitely ahead of me on the trail. What are you getting at?"

Lieutenant Landau smiled with satisfaction and leaned back in her chair. Swiftly she drew a packet of cigarettes out of her purse and lit one with a quick stroke of a match. Then she inhaled deeply and smiled at KC again. "You were quite close to Brooks that afternoon, weren't you, KC?" she said.

"No," KC said coldly. The smoke rose into her eyes, stinging them.

"There are two trails that lead to the cliff Mr. Baldwin fell off. You know that, don't you?"

"What?" KC said slowly.

"It was *you* Brooks heard that afternoon, not Angela Beth," the police woman went on, taking another drag on the cigarette, then exhaling. "It was *you* he was trying to run from."

"It was *you* Mr. Baldwin was afraid of."

"Afraid . . .?" KC whispered, staring in horror at Lieutenant Landau's sharp face and penciled eyebrows.

"You'd just threatened him in front of a large crowd at the picnic," the lieutenant growled. "Come on. Admit it."

"Admit *what*?" KC heard herself shout. A rush of hot blood flooded her face. "Aren't you supposed to be some—some kind of *professional*?" she heard herself shout. With both hands, she wildly waved away the curl of cigarette smoke drifting toward her face.

Lieutenant Landau drew back, nodding. She gave KC a satisfied smile, then took a deep drag. "Tell me, KC. Is this what usually happens when you get angry?"

"I—I," KC sputtered.

Lieutenant Landau's eyes glinted with victory. She shook her head. "Did you lose your temper on the mountain with your friend, Brooks, too?"

"Stop it!" KC yelled.

"You probably didn't really mean to push Brooks, did you? You were just angry with him and you couldn't control—"

"Push?" KC repeated. "Push *who*? Push *Brooks*? What are you talking about?"

Suddenly, the lieutenant's face turned to stone. She twisted in her seat and drew her face so near, KC thought her beaklike nose was going to poke her. "You better tell us everything. And tell us now. We have a witness claiming she saw you push Brooks Baldwin from a ledge on Mount Crinsley. And we have dozens of others who heard you threaten him less than an hour before he died."

"No!" KC shouted back, shaking her head. "You're crazy."

☎

1 (800) I LUV BKS!

If you'd like to hear more about your
favorite young adult novels and writers . . .
OR
If you'd like to tell us what you thought
of this book or other books
you've recently read . . .

CALL US at 1(800) I LUV BKS
[1(800) 458-8257]

Monday to Friday, 9AM – 8PM EST

You'll hear a new message about books and
other interesting subjects each month.

**The call is free, but please get
your parents' permission first.**